LIFE SUPPORT

Jennifer Taylor

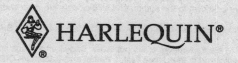

HARLEQUIN®

TORONTO • NEW YORK • LONDON
AMSTERDAM • PARIS • SYDNEY • HAMBURG
STOCKHOLM • ATHENS • TOKYO • MILAN • MADRID
PRAGUE • WARSAW • BUDAPEST • AUCKLAND

ISBN 0-373-51261-9

LIFE SUPPORT

First North American Publication 2003

Copyright © 2002 by Jennifer Taylor

This edition published by arrangement with Harlequin Books S.A.

® and TM are trademarks of the publisher. Trademarks indicated with ® are registered in the United States Patent and Trademark Office, the Canadian Trade Marks Office and in other countries.

Visit us at www.eHarlequin.com

Printed in U.S.A.

Jennifer Taylor lives in the northwest of England with her husband, Bill. She had been writing Harlequin romances for some years, but when she discovered Medical Romances, she was so captivated by these heartwarming stories that she set out to write them herself! When not writing or doing research for her latest book, Jennifer's hobbies include reading, travel, walking her dog and retail therapy (shopping!). Jennifer claims all that bending and stretching to reach the shelves is the best exercise possible.

GLOSSARY

A and E—accident and emergency department

B and G—bloods and glucose

Consultant—nd experienced specialist registrar who is the leader of a medical team; there can be a junior and senior consultant on a team

CVA—cerebrovascular accident

Duty registrar—the doctor on call

FBC—full blood count

Fixator—an external device, a kind of frame, for rigidly holding bones together while they heal

GA—general anesthetic

GCS—the Glasgow Coma Scale, used to determine a patient's level of consciousness

Houseman/house officer—British equivalent of a medical intern or clerk

MI—myocardial infarction

Obs—observations re: pulse, blood pressure, etc.

Registrar/specialist registrar—a doctor who is trained in a particular area of medicine

Resus—room or unit where a patient is taken for resuscitation after cardiac accident

Rostered—scheduled

RTA—road traffic accident

Senior House Officer (SHO)—British equivalent of a resident

Theatre—operating room

CHAPTER ONE

'WHAT we're hoping for is some sort of big emergency. A multiple car crash would be great! We want to grab the viewers by the scruffs of their necks and stop them reaching for their remote controls and changing channels.'

'I'm surprised you haven't thought about it before, Hugh, and set something up.'

Dominic Walsh tilted back his chair and placed his elegantly shod feet on the edge of the desk. There was a sardonic gleam in his green eyes as he noted the fervent expression on the other man's face.

They were sitting in a trailer that had been parked on the forecourt of St Justin's Hospital in London. All around them there was a hive of activity as the crew prepared for that week's episode of *Health Matters*, the country's top-rated medical show. Today was the opening of the hospital's newly refurbished Accident and Emergency unit and the show's producers had decided that they would spend the day there.

There were half a dozen live broadcasts scheduled throughout the day, plus regular updates on any patients who were treated. As the host of the show, Dominic was confident that it would draw a wide audience, although he wasn't sure if he agreed with the decision to spend so much time in the unit. The staff would be trying to find their feet, and the last thing he wanted was to make life more difficult for them.

'Surely it wouldn't be that difficult to stage an accident so you can get the effect you want?' he suggested drily.

'No, no, that's the whole point! We want real-life drama, the cutting edge of accident and emergency care as it happens. God forbid that our audience should think we're faking it!'

Hugh glanced round distractedly as one of the crew stuck his head round the door to tell him there was a problem with the lighting. He seemed unaware that Dominic's suggestion hadn't been a serious one. 'I'll have to go and sort that out. Here's a list of the staff you'll be interviewing. They've all agreed to co-operate, apart from the senior registrar. She's made it clear that she wants nothing to do with the show.'

Dominic frowned as he glanced at the clipboard Hugh had given him and saw a red line scored through one of the names. 'So what's Dr Michelle Roberts got against becoming a television star?'

'No idea,' Hugh replied as he grabbed a wad of notes off the desk. He hurried to the door then stopped and glanced back.

'Any chance you could try a bit of the famous Walsh charm on the lady, Dominic? She's quite a looker from all accounts and she could be a big draw for the male members of our audience if you could persuade her to co-operate.'

'I'll try, but I'm not promising anything.' Dominic swung his feet to the floor and stood up. 'She might be a man-hater for all we know.'

'Well, if you can't talk her round then nobody can,' Hugh replied cheerfully as he made a hurried exit.

Dominic sighed as he followed Hugh out of the van. He still wasn't comfortable with the idea that he had become the nation's latest heart-throb. Oh, he was realistic enough to know that his looks had helped enormously when he'd decided to change track a couple of years ago and opt for this type of work.

The fact that he was six feet tall, leanly built with black hair and what one tabloid journalist had termed a 'killer smile' had definitely worked in his favour. However, he hated the thought that what he did might get trivialised because of it, and that people might not realise the true purpose behind *Health Matters*. Raising public awareness of the need for good health care had always been his main aim.

He shrugged aside the thought as he made his way to the A and E department. Although it wouldn't be opened officially for another half-hour, there was quite a crowd already gathered in the waiting area. His arrival caused a bit of a stir and he stopped a number of times to sign autographs for several of the people who were waiting to be seen.

'I just love your show, Dr Walsh. I never miss an episode.'

'Thank you.' He quickly signed his name on the scrap of paper the elderly woman had presented him with, then frowned in concern when he noticed the gash on her forehead. 'How did you do that?'

'I tripped over the cat,' she explained ruefully. 'Silly of me, wasn't it? Do you think it will need stitching?'

'Well, I'm—' Dominic had been about to say that he was sure the doctor would decide on the best course of treatment when a cool, female voice suddenly forestalled him.

'I think we should wait until we've examined you, Mrs MacFarland, before we decide if you need stitches. The nurse will call you through very shortly.'

Dominic swung round but the woman who had spoken

to them had already walked away. He just caught a glimpse of a rigidly straight back and the most wonderful pair of legs he'd ever had the good fortune to see before she disappeared into one of the treatment rooms.

He quickly handed over the autograph, excused himself and went to the reception desk, wondering why that fleeting glimpse should have made his skin prickle in such a peculiar fashion. It felt as though a current of static electricity had suddenly passed through his system, and although it wasn't an unpleasant feeling it surprised him enough to want to know a little more about the woman who had caused such a reaction.

'I'm Dominic Walsh,' he began, but the middle-aged receptionist didn't give him a chance to finish introducing himself.

'I know! Oh, I just *love* your programme, Dr Walsh. It's absolutely the best thing on television!'

'Thank you.' Dominic glanced at the identity badge pinned to her blouse. 'I wonder if you could help me, Trisha? Who was that woman who spoke to me just now?'

'Oh, that was Dr Roberts. She's the senior registrar in A and E.' The receptionist lowered her voice confidingly. 'Actually, she was offered the consultancy post after we were refurbished, but she turned it down. Said that she didn't want to have to waste her time playing politics.'

'Really? That is interesting.'

Dominic smiled, although it was an effort to hide his surprise. Few doctors would turn down the chance of a consultancy in this day and age when it meant missing out on all the perks that went with the job. Not that he didn't sympathise with her, of course. In his experience, the higher up the ladder you climbed, the more time you

spent fighting for staffing and funding, or whatever else
was on the agenda.

It was one of the main reasons why he had opted out
of hands-on medicine, in fact. If he was going to do
anything to improve the country's health-care system he
needed to concentrate all his energies on that, rather than
trying to split himself in two all the time.

Still, it did make him see that it could be interesting
if Dr Roberts could be persuaded to air her views on
live television. Although Hugh had said that she wasn't
keen to appear on the show, he was confident that he
would be able to change her mind with a little gentle
encouragement.

'I'd really love to talk to Dr Roberts, Trisha. Do you
think she would agree to be interviewed?'

'I'm not sure about that.' Trisha looked a little embarrassed. 'Dr Roberts wasn't very keen on having you
here, I'm afraid. She said that the last thing people need
when they're ill is a television camera being pointed at
them.'

'We shall be very discreet,' he assured her. 'And nobody will be filmed without their permission. Maybe Dr
Roberts just needs a bit of reassurance. I'll have a word
with her as soon as she's free.'

Dominic smiled his thanks then quickly made his way
across the waiting room. The camera crew were rigging
up the lighting outside the new resuscitation room and
he glanced inside as he passed. No expense had been
spared and the equipment was state of the art. It was
heartening to know that so many people would benefit
from the new facilities, and rewarding to realise that he
had played a major part in securing the funding for the
project. It was proof, if he had needed it, that he had
made the right decision by switching tracks.

He saw the door to the treatment room opening and quickened his pace, wanting to slip in and speak to Dr Roberts before the next patient was summoned. There was a young, blonde-haired nurse showing out the last patient and she gasped when she recognised him.

'You're Dominic Walsh, aren't you?'

'I am indeed.' He treated her to his famous smile. 'Is there any chance I could have a quick word with Dr Roberts? I promise I won't take more than a couple of seconds.'

'Oh, I don't know...' The young nurse glanced uncertainly over her shoulder then shrugged. 'Well, I suppose it will be all right.'

'Thanks.' Dominic grinned as he sped past her. At any other time he might have taken a little more time to thank her properly because she was very pretty, but he needed to get this interview arranged as soon as he could. Dr Roberts's views could make for an interesting show and that was what mattered most.

'If you would take a seat I'll be right with you.'

He paused at the sound of that coolly refined voice. Dr Roberts was at the sink, washing her hands, and she didn't look round as she plucked a paper towel from the dispenser. 'It's Mrs MacFarland, isn't it?'

'I'm afraid not.'

Dominic laughed apologetically when he saw her jump. 'Sorry. I didn't mean to startle you. I just wondered if I could have a quick word before you see your next patient,' he began, then found his voice drying up when she turned round and he got his first proper look at her.

He felt a tiny pulsing begin in the pit of his stomach as he took rapid stock of a porcelain-fine complexion, smoky-grey eyes and a wonderfully mobile mouth. They were the first things he noticed but his eyes weren't slow to drink in all the other fascinating details.

Her hair was a very dark brown. Although he wasn't an expert on hair colours, he would have classed it as sable. It was drawn severely back from her face and pinned into a no-nonsense knot at the nape of her neck, but he just knew that it would be wonderfully thick and soft to the touch.

She was simply dressed in a blue shirt and a black wool skirt under her starched white coat, but he could tell that her figure was both trim and curvaceous. His delighted gaze was just about to make its way down so that he could check if her legs really were as fabulous as he remembered them to be when she spoke and he froze when he heard the icy note of displeasure in her voice.

'I have already made it perfectly clear that I do not wish to be interviewed. Now, if you will excuse me, I have patients waiting.'

She flung the paper towel into the waste sack then stalked to the door. Dominic sucked in his breath as he realised that she was virtually ordering him out of the room. Frankly, it was a situation that he hadn't encountered before, but he wasn't going to let that deter him.

'I know how busy you are, Dr Roberts, and I promise that I won't take up too much of your time. However, I've just learned that you turned down the offer of a consultant's post. I'm sure our viewers would be interested to hear you talking about your reasons for refusing the job.'

'Why? What possible good could it do them to know why I turned down the job?'

She smiled thinly, her beautiful mouth curling cynically at the corners. 'Do you really think it will reassure the public to learn that fifty per cent of an A and E consultant's time is spent arguing with fund managers for more money? Will they honestly feel better if I tell them that because of that more often than not the doctor who provides their emergency care has less than a year's experience? I doubt that will create the kind of feel-good factor you're hoping to promote on your programme.'

'*Health Matters* isn't in the business of making people feel good,' he shot back, stung by the accusation. 'It's a programme that aims to educate people about every-thing to do with their health, and by doing so improve the whole health care system.'

'Really? I shall have to take your word for that, Mr Walsh, because I've never watched the show. Unfortunately, I'm usually too busy working to watch television.' She glanced over her shoulder and nodded to the nurse. 'Call in the next patient, please, Amy. I'm sure Mr Walsh understands how busy we are and will excuse us.'

'Of course. But you're taking a very blinkered view, Dr Roberts. Publicity can and does make a huge differ-ence.' He paused on his way out, feeling more rattled than he'd felt in ages. He didn't see why he should feel that he had to defend himself yet that was exactly what he was doing.

The thought angered him but he didn't let his feelings show as he treated her to a deliberately warm smile. 'Anyway, thank you for your time, Dr Roberts. If there's anything I can ever do for you, please, don't hesitate to get in touch. Oh, and by the way, it's *Dr* Walsh, just so you know for future reference. Funnily enough, I worked in accident and emergency care as well, so that's some-thing we have in common.'

'What a shame that you saw fit to sell out, *Dr* Walsh.

We have few enough doctors as it is, especially in emergency care. That's one of the main reasons why the system is in such a deplorable state.'

She looked him straight in the eye and Dominic couldn't fail to see the contempt on her face. 'We need people actually *doing* the work, not making television programmes about it. That's the only way we'll ever make any improvements.'

She turned and went back inside without giving him a chance to reply. Dominic's mouth set into a grim line as he strode across the waiting room. Maybe it was silly to let her comments get to him, but he had rarely encountered that kind of attitude since he'd launched the show. Most medics he spoke to were only too happy to be offered the chance to air their views on national television, and co-operated fully. So why didn't Michelle Roberts feel the same?

Just for a second, he found himself wondering if she had been right. Would he have achieved more if he'd continued working in medicine? He'd told himself that this was the only way he would ever improve the system, but *had* it been the easy way out?

It was an unsettling thought and he was glad when Hugh appeared to tell him that they would be on air in five minutes' time. Dominic went to get ready, taking his place by the main doors of the unit in preparation for the opening credits.

He squared his shoulders as Hugh began the countdown and the show's theme music began to play. To hell with it. If Michelle Roberts didn't want to co-operate, that was her choice. He certainly wasn't going to shed any tears over her decision!

'Michelle was really awful to him. She told him that he had sold out by choosing to work in television. I know she made no secret of the fact that she was against the idea of having the camera crew here, but I couldn't believe she'd be so rude, especially when Dominic Walsh is so lovely!'

Michelle paused as she caught the tail end of the conversation. The staffroom door was slightly ajar, otherwise she might not have heard what the nurse had been saying. Now she frowned as she thought back to what had happened earlier that morning. Had she perhaps been a bit hard on Dominic Walsh?

The uncertainty lasted no more than ten seconds before she dismissed it. Of course she hadn't! Anyone who was prepared to squander years of expensive training, as he had done, deserved all he got.

'Any tea left in the pot?' she asked, walking into the room. She saw young Amy Carlisle blush and sighed. 'Yes, Amy, I heard what you said in case you're wondering. I'm sorry if you think I was a bit rough on Dominic Walsh, but he's big enough to take it. I certainly don't imagine that he'll have been broken-hearted because I refused to co-operate.'

'I suppose not.' Amy obviously decided that it would be better not to say anything else, and quickly shoved the pot across the table. She was one of their new recruits and was still finding her feet. 'There should be a drop of tea left but it's probably stewed by now, I'm afraid.'

'I'll make some more,' Michelle offered, going to the sink to fill the kettle. 'Do you want another cup, Ruth?'

'No, I'd better get back.' Ruth Humphries, another nurse on the unit, grimaced as she got up. She was one of the old staff who had asked to return to the unit after the refurbishment. 'Max has had me fetching and carrying for him all morning long. I hope he isn't going to carry on like that or I'll be sorely tempted to tell him where to get off!'

Michelle sighed. She'd had reservations when she'd heard that Max Hastings had been offered the consultant's post after she'd turned it down. Whilst she didn't doubt his ability to do the job, he did have a tendency to expect the staff to cater to his every whim.

'It's probably first day nerves,' she said lightly, hoping to defuse the situation. If they were going to work together successfully as a team, they all had to be pulling in the same direction. It wouldn't help one bit if Max started lording it over the rest of the staff.

'Either that or he's stage-struck.' Ruth rolled her eyes as she made for the door. 'I heard him asking the camera crew to make sure they got his best side, would you believe? Maybe he's hoping that he'll get an offer from Hollywood after today is over!'

'Who knows?' Michelle laughed but she couldn't deny that it irritated her that the filming was creating such havoc.

She emptied away the dregs of tea and rinsed the pot, thinking back over the busy morning they'd had. They'd had far more patients turning up that day than she'd expected, even allowing for the fact that the reopening of the unit had attracted a great deal of publicity locally. A lot of the people she had seen had presented with very minor injuries as well, which would have been dealt with by their general practitioners normally.

There was little doubt in her mind that Dominic Walsh's decision to present his show from St Justin's had been the main cause, and it was another black mark against him in her opinion. Anyone with an ounce of common sense should have realised that the last thing they had needed today of all days was a media circus!

It wasn't like her to think such sour thoughts so she tried to put them out of her mind while she had her break. She had just popped a couple of fresh teabags into the pot when Ruth poked her head round the door.

'Sorry, Michelle, but can you come? Ambulance Control has phoned to say they've picked up a girl in town. Heavy vaginal bleeding and in a pretty bad state.'

'Of course. Where's Max got to?' Michelle abandoned her tea-making and hurriedly followed Ruth back to the unit.

'He's doing an interview with Dominic Walsh.' Ruth shrugged. 'He said to ask you to deal with this because he was busy.'

'Fine.'

Michelle's mouth snapped shut. It wasn't her place to comment on the new head of department's decisions, not that she blamed Max, of course. Maybe Dominic Walsh's fans believed that he was performing a public service, but she wasn't so gullible. The only interests dear to *Dr* Walsh's heart had his name stamped all over them.

The ambulance arrived a few minutes later and she hurried out to meet it. The television crew must have got wind of what was happening because there were a couple of cameramen outside, filming as the paramedics unloaded the trolley.

Michelle caught a glimpse of Dominic Walsh hurrying towards her and deliberately turned her back on him. Frankly, she didn't need any distractions while she was dealing with a patient.

'What do we know so far?' she asked as she hurried

alongside the stretcher as the paramedics wheeled it inside.

'Not much,' Bill Trent, one of their most senior ambulance crew, told her. 'She had no identification on her and we've no idea how long she'd been lying in the alley. A couple of kids trying to sneak in through the back door of the cinema found her apparently. She's obviously lost a lot of blood so we started her on fluids straight away. She was unconscious when she was found and we've not been able to get a response from her on the way here.'

'Right. Take her straight through to Resus while we have a look.'

Michelle hurried on ahead, grabbing hold of one of the doors as the paramedics pushed the trolley into the resuscitation room. She looked round as Ruth handed her a plastic apron and gloves. 'Thanks.'

She quickly got kitted up then lifted back the blanket and frowned in dismay when she saw the amount of blood that had pooled on the sheet between the girl's legs. 'Very severe blood loss. What's her blood pressure?'

'Not good,' Ruth reported, checking the girl's blood pressure reading. 'Seventy over forty, and it's dropping fast.'

'Get a second line in and someone take a blood sample and get the lab to cross-match it, stat!' Michelle rapped out, bending to examine the girl.

The rest of the resus team had arrived now and were taking their places around the bed. She often thought it was like a well-rehearsed dance routine, with everyone knowing their steps. When it worked well it was wonderful; when it didn't chaos ensued. She had spent a lot of time drilling everyone prior to the reopening of the unit and it paid off now, leaving her free to concentrate on the patient rather than all the routine procedures.

The girl was Asian and looked to be in her mid-teens, certainly no older than eighteen. Michelle quickly checked her over for any obvious signs of injury while Kate Morris cut away the clothing from the lower half of her body, but she seemed to be fine apart from the massive bleeding.

She moved to the bottom of the bed as soon as Kate had finished, carefully checking the girl's vaginal passage and then palpating her abdomen. She sighed when she realised that her suspicions had been correct.

'She's recently given birth. I can feel parts of the placenta that have been left behind.'

'Post-partum haemorrhage,' a deep voice suggested.

Michelle glanced round and frowned when she realised that Dominic Walsh had followed them into the resuscitation room. 'What are you doing in here?'

'Max said it would be OK. Naturally, we won't use any footage we shoot without the patient's permission.'

His green eyes challenged her to argue with him but Michelle didn't have the time to spare. The best she could do was treat him to a look that should have stopped him in his tracks if he'd had a shred of decency in his body.

She turned to Ruth. 'Get onto the obstetrics registrar and ask him to come down here a.s.a.p. She's going to need a Dilatation and Curettage to get rid of all the debris and stitching from the look of things. There's extensive vaginal tearing, which isn't helping matters.'

'What about the baby?'

Michelle paused and looked round. Dominic Walsh was standing so close to her that she could see the tiny golden flecks in his green eyes. All of a sudden something odd seemed to happen to her heart, as though it had fitted in two beats where one would have done. It was such a peculiar sensation that she had difficulty thinking clearly for a second and frowned when he repeated the question.

'What's happened to the baby? If it's post-partum haemorrhage then where is the child?' His tone was clipped, the indolent note she'd heard in it moments earlier having completely disappeared. 'She must have given birth fairly recently from the look of her, so that means there's a baby out there somewhere. We need to find it—fast.'

'Of course.' Michelle's mind cleared and she frowned. 'I'll get onto the police and ask them to look for it. It's possible that someone is taking care of it, of course.'

'Highly doubtful, if you want my opinion, Dr Roberts,' Dominic replied harshly. Michelle was shocked when she saw the anger in his eyes as he looked at the girl. 'If anyone had been looking after this kid, they wouldn't have let her get into this state. Where was she found?'

'In an alley off the high street, close to the cinema, I believe.'

It took her all her time to respond with an outward show of calm. Maybe it was silly but she had never imagined that Dominic Walsh would let anything affect him this much. It seemed to push the mental image she had formed of him slightly askew, and that bothered her. A lot.

She jumped when he swung round and headed for the door. 'Where are you going?'

'To see if I can find the baby.' His tone was so grim that everyone in the room fell silent. 'I can't just wait around here and leave it up to the police. Not even *I* can do that, Dr Roberts. This is one occasion when I'm forced to adopt a hands-on policy, you'll be surprised to know!'

He left the room with the camera crew scurrying after him. Michelle heard a collective sigh go up and only then realised that everyone had been holding their breath. She summoned a shaky smile but her legs felt like jelly all of a sudden and she had the most ridiculous urge to cry.

'I think I have just been well and truly put in my place.'

Everyone laughed but she could tell that her colleagues believed she had been wrong to write off Dominic Walsh the way she had. It was more than a little disquieting to realise it on top of what had just happened.

Was it possible that she *had* misjudged him?

'For heavens sake, Dominic, you can't just walk out of here!'

'No? Watch me!'

Dominic strode across the car park, thanking his lucky stars that he had driven himself to the hospital that morning. Maybe he was wrong to see this as some kind of personal test, but he couldn't help it. If anything happened to that baby...

He cut off the thought because it wouldn't help. Hugh was almost beside himself with dismay and he spared him a grim smile. 'We've got twenty minutes before we're back on air. I'm hoping to be back by then.'

'And what if you're not? What are we going to do then? Please, Dominic, I beg you to leave this to the police! They'll find the baby.'

'Maybe they will, but I'm still going. Sorry, Hugh, there's no point arguing because I've made up my mind.'

He slid into the driving seat and gunned the engine.

Hugh stepped smartly out of the way as Dominic pulled out of the bay. He had done a lot of research on this area of London prior to the show, so he was able to guess with a fair degree of accuracy where they had found the girl. It took him just over ten minutes to get there because of the traffic, and the police were already there when he arrived.

Dominic parked his car, sighing when he saw two of the crew draw up behind him. It was typical of Hugh not to let any opportunity pass him by!

He was just crossing the road when he heard a shout go up and saw a couple of policemen running along the road. Dominic raced after them, pushing his way through the crowd that had started to gather outside the public toilets. One of the police officers was kneeling on the pavement, bending over the tiny form of a baby. Dominic's heart leapt into his throat as he hurried forward and crouched down beside them.

'Let me see. I'm a doctor,' he said curtly.

It was a baby boy, very small but perfectly formed. Placing his ear to the child's chest, he tried to hear if there was a heartbeat, but there was too much noise going on in the street. He placed his fingers against the baby's neck to see if he could find a pulse and felt a surge of relief rush through him when he detected a tiny throbbing.

'He's alive but we need to get him to hospital straight away.' Stripping off his jacket, he quickly wrapped the baby in it and stood up, cradling the tiny form against him so that his own body heat would help to warm it up. Although it was May and fairly warm, a newborn baby lost its body heat so rapidly that already hypothermia might have set in. The child had been wrapped in a towel but it would have provided little insulation. The thought that the baby might have survived this long yet not make it was more than he could bear.

The crowd parted seemingly by magic as he strode across the pavement with the infant nestled in his arms. An ambulance had arrived and he went straight to it and climbed into the back.

'We need to get some fluids into him, stat!' he ordered. 'He's dehydrated and very cold.'

'We've got some already warmed,' the young woman paramedic told him. 'And we've brought a heat pad because Dr Roberts explained that it was a neonate.'

'Good.' Dominic spared her a smile as he placed the baby on the warmed blankets and tucked them around him. 'We'll need the smallest-bore cannula you've got to get a line in.'

'This do?' She handed him a tiny plastic tube. Inside it contained a sharply pointed rod called a trocar that would be used to puncture the infant's vein. Once that was removed they would be able to run fluids into his body through the tube.

'That's perfect.'

Dominic realised that he was holding his breath as he set up the line. It had been a while since he had worked with veins this minute but he hadn't lost his touch, he was relieved to see. He attached a bag of warmed fluid to the tubing and grinned with delight as he watched the first drops flow into the tiny body.

'Piece of cake, really.'

The young paramedic laughed. 'Or good old-fashioned skill. I'm glad *I* didn't have to get a line into a vein that small!'

It didn't take them long to get back to the hospital. The police had provided an escort and they sped through the traffic. Dominic picked up the baby as soon as the ambulance had stopped and carried him outside. There was quite a crowd gathered in front of the A and E department, and Hugh had the cameras rolling, but he ignored everything as he hurried inside.

Michelle met him outside the resuscitation room and he could see the worry in her beautiful grey eyes. 'How is he?'

'Cold but alive. Thanks for sending along that heat pad and everything. It's helped enormously.'

He carried the baby into the room and laid him on the bed, then gently unwrapped the blankets and peeled back the folds of his jacket. 'He seems unharmed, mercifully enough. Pulse is faint but it's got stronger on the way here. The fluids have helped, that and being warmed up.'

He smoothed a gentle hand over the child's head, feeling a lump come to his throat. 'At least he has a chance now, and that's something.'

'It is.'

He glanced round when he heard the catch in her voice and was surprised when he saw tears trembling on her lashes. 'Hey, come on, now. Don't get upset. He's going to make it.'

'Do you think so?'

She looked up and Dominic felt as though someone had punched him hard in the stomach as she looked at him with swimming eyes. All of a sudden he knew that he would move heaven and earth if it meant that he could take away the worry he saw on her face.

'Yes, I do.' He took hold of her hands and held them tightly, wanting some of his certainty to rub off on her because he couldn't bear to see her looking so upset. 'He's going to live, Michelle. I promise you that.'

He had barely finished speaking when the door suddenly opened and Hugh came hurrying into the room.

'Brilliant idea of yours, Dominic! I don't know why I didn't realise what you were up to.'

'I'm sorry?' Dominic looked at him in confusion. He felt Michelle quickly withdraw her hands and wondered at the sense of loss he felt when her slender fingers were removed from his grasp.

'Rushing off like that to find the babe, of course!'

Hugh beamed with pleasure as he looked at the child. 'The public is going to lap this up. Just wait until they see the footage we shot of you. They'll love the idea of their favourite TV medico being the hero of the hour!'

'Oh, but I...' Dominic got no further as Hugh clapped him on the shoulder and hurried away. He took a deep breath but he knew what was going to greet him before he even looked at Michelle. His heart sank when he saw the disdain on her beautiful face.

'Congratulations, Dr Walsh. Not many people get themselves classed as a hero simply by looking after their own interests.'

'It wasn't like that,' he denied, although he didn't know why he was bothering to try and convince her. *He* knew that self-glorification had been the last thing on his mind when he had rushed off to find the baby, and that should have been enough. Yet he felt this deep need to set matters straight.

'Wasn't it?' She looked round as the door opened and a nurse came in with a portable incubator. 'I'd ask you to explain if I had the time or the inclination, but unfortunately I have neither. There are patients waiting to be seen and you have your adoring public wanting to pay homage. I hope you enjoy the rest of your day here, Dr Walsh.'

With that she turned her back on him. Dominic sucked

in an angry breath but he'd be damned if he would let her see how much her comments had stung.

He strode out of the room and almost ran into Hugh who had been coming to find him. It was time for the next broadcast and Hugh intended to run the film of the baby being found.

Dominic checked through the script that had been hastily prepared, cutting out the more effusive passages, the ones that showed him in the most favourable light. He hadn't gone looking for the child either for personal gain or public recognition, and he intended to make that clear. Not that there was a hope in hell that one particular person would believe it!

CHAPTER TWO

By SEVEN o'clock that night Michelle was flagging. She made her way to the staffroom and sank onto a chair, too tired even to make herself a cup of coffee.

She had been on duty since six that morning and wouldn't be leaving work until at least ten p.m. It was her own fault because she should have insisted that Max hire a temporary replacement when the new junior registrar they'd appointed had informed them that he'd broken his ankle and wouldn't be able to start until the middle of the following month.

Instead she had allowed Max to persuade her that they would be able to manage with agency staff. Ever mindful of the budget, and how badly it would reflect on him if they got off to a bad start, he had been eager to reduce their overheads. It wouldn't have been a problem if he had got straight onto the agency, but he had left it until yesterday to contact them, with predictable results.

They'd had nobody on their books either available or willing to work. The accident and emergency department of any hospital was one of the toughest places to work and few agency doctors willingly opted for it. It meant that she would be working double shifts for the next month, not that it was anything unusual. It might be a brand-new unit, but there were still the same old problems to contend with.

She glanced round as the door opened and John Peterson, their new houseman—intern—came into the room. 'Hi, how are you doing?'

'I feel as though my head is spinning,' he confessed.

He was a rather earnest looking young man in his mid-twenties and had just completed his studies at medical school. Michelle knew how hard he would find it for the first few months because it was a shock to be pushed out into the big wide world after the security of university.

'It will take you a couple of weeks to settle in,' she consoled him. 'It's a bit of shock at first when you have to deal with real patients.'

'I know. I've been dreading it because I found it really hard whenever we did a stint on the wards.' John grimaced as he plugged in the kettle. 'I never really know what to say to people. They teach you all the theory at med school but they can't teach you that bit.'

'You'll get better with practice. And usually we're so rushed in this department that folk don't get the time to decide if we have a good bedside manner. It's wheel them in and wheel them out, I'm afraid!'

John laughed. 'I suppose that's one advantage to working here. How's that baby doing, by the way? I saw the broadcast just before I came on duty this afternoon. It was a damned good job that Dominic Walsh was there when they found the child. He probably saved the poor little thing's life.'

'The baby is fine,' Michelle said quickly, not wanting to be drawn into a discussion about Walsh's input into the child's recovery.

She was still having problems coming to terms with how disappointed she'd felt when she'd realised that it had all been a publicity stunt. The fact that she had allowed herself to be taken in by Walsh's apparent concern was something else that had stuck in her throat. He had to be a consummate actor because he'd had her fooled.

'I phoned the neonatal unit about an hour ago and they were very pleased with him. He's taken a feed and he seems quite alert so they're pretty confident that he should be all right.'

'Are you talking about the baby we found?'

Michelle looked round when she heard Dominic Walsh's deep voice. The camera crew were still filming and would remain in the unit all night, although she didn't expect he would stay that long. There was just one more broadcast scheduled for eight o'clock so he would probably leave after it was over.

'Don't you mean the baby *you* found? Credit where it's due, Dr Walsh.'

He treated her to a cool smile as he sat down but she could see the glint of anger in his eyes. For some reason it pleased her enormously to know that she had needled him.

'I really can't claim all the credit, Dr Roberts. I was merely one small cog in the wheel, you might say.'

'Tut-tut, you're too modest, Dr Walsh!'

She smiled tauntingly, wondering why she felt this need to make him understand that he hadn't fooled her even if the rest of the country was hailing him as a hero. She had caught a glimpse of the evening news and the story about the baby's rescue—and his part in the proceedings—had been made much of.

'Why, who knows what might have happened without your intervention?'

'I imagine the paramedics would have simply got on with the job,' he said flatly. 'And does it really matter who did what at the end of the day? So long as the child is all right, that's the main thing.'

Michelle felt a little colour touch her cheeks when she heard the rebuke in his voice. Even though she hated to admit it, she knew that it had been justified.

She stood up, suddenly uncomfortable with the way she had been behaving. It wasn't like her to act like that and certainly not in her nature to deny anyone the credit due to them. No matter what his motives might have been, Dominic Walsh *had* saved the baby's life and it wasn't fair of her to belittle what he had done.

'You're quite right, of course, Dr Walsh. It doesn't really matter who saved the child's life, but that doesn't mean you didn't do a good job.'

She saw the surprise in his eyes and felt her heart slip in an extra beat again when he suddenly smiled at her. 'Thank you, Michelle. It means a lot to hear you say that.'

'You're welcome.'

She swung round and headed for the door, wondering why she felt a sudden need to put some distance between them. Was it the fact that when Dominic had smiled at her like that she had been sorely tempted to say something else nice to him?

The thought that she was so weak-willed that she had been swayed by his charm annoyed her intensely and she saw Helen Andrews, the new night nurse, look at her in surprise as she walked past the desk.

'Is something wrong, Dr Roberts?'

'No, no. I was just miles away.' She gave the woman a sickly smile. 'So how are you settling in, Helen? I'm sorry that I haven't had much time to speak to you yet, but it's been so busy.'

'You can say that again! I thought things would have started to tail off by now, but we've still got a queue of people waiting to be seen. I should have known we'd be packed out as soon as I heard that Dominic Walsh was presenting this week's edition of *Health Matters* from here.'

Helen sighed dreamily. 'I still can't believe that I've actually met him. I have to be his biggest fan!'

'Really?' Michelle felt as though her smile were glued into place. 'So you've not found it a bit of nuisance, having the cameramen here?'

'Oh, definitely not! And Dominic is so considerate. He goes out of his way to put you at ease...' Helen broke off and laughed self-consciously. 'Oops, your ears must be burning. We were just talking about you.'

'Something nice, I hope?'

Dominic strolled over to join them and Michelle stiffened when she felt his arm brushing hers. She skimmed him a warning look as she stepped away, but he ignored it as he treated her and Helen to a charming smile.

'Would it be wise to ask what you were saying about me?'

'Better not,' she advised sweetly. 'That way you won't run the risk of being disappointed, will you?'

'Oh, I doubt I'd ever be disappointed by what you said, Michelle. I'd need to have certain expectations before I could have them dashed.'

'How wise of you to take that realistic view,' she shot back.

'I always prefer to know exactly where I stand.'

He folded his arms and regarded her thoughtfully, one black brow crooking as he studied her set face. 'So come along, Michelle, out with it. What precisely have you got against me?'

'I'm sorry, Dr Walsh, but I really don't have the time to spare to play puerile games.'

'Scared that you might have to revise your opinion of

me?' he taunted. 'It nearly choked you just now to admit that I might have helped to save that baby's life, didn't it? Obviously, you've got some kind of a bee in your bonnet about me so don't be shy—spit it out.'

'Very well, but don't blame me if you don't like what you hear. It can be dangerous to believe your own publicity, Dr Walsh. What's that term that's all the vogue nowadays... Ah, yes, spin-doctoring.'

She laughed softly when she saw his eyes darken. Suddenly, she forgot where they were and the fact that there were people listening. 'Anyone can create the right image with a little help, but it doesn't mean there's anything to back it up.'

'So, basically, what you are saying is that I lack substance? And that the work I do isn't important?'

She felt a shiver run through her when she heard the dark note in his voice. It was obvious that he was furiously angry even though he was making an effort to disguise it. A tiny voice of reason was urging her not to pursue the conversation but she refused to listen to it. As far as she was concerned, he had committed the very worst of crimes by abandoning his medical career for the sake of material gain.

'That's right. If you were really serious about wanting to help people, you wouldn't be wasting all those years you spent training. A lot of time and money was invested in you, Dr Walsh, and for what? So that you can appear on national television and feed the public a lot of anodyne nonsense?'

'If people don't know what's available to them then they won't know what to ask for,' he shot back. 'Raise their expectations of the kind of health care they should be receiving and they'll demand a better service. It's the only way that we'll make improvements.'

'And you really think it's that simple? You tell people what they need and—hey presto—someone waves a magic wand and everything is wonderful,' she taunted.

'No, it isn't that simple, as you very well know,' he stated with such authority that she fell silent. 'Improving our health-care system costs money. Some of the areas which are most desperately in need of funding are the ones that don't always attract the interest of the politicians. Take this department, for example. The plans for refurbishing St Justin's A and E department were drawn up years ago, but there was never enough money until *Health Matters* stepped in and found investors.'

She hadn't known about his involvement and it threw her for a moment, but not enough to make her back down. 'Obviously we should be grateful to you, then, Dr Walsh. Is that what you want—people's thanks?' She shrugged, a tiny smile curling her mouth as she stared into his angry green eyes. 'Thank you, we're very grateful for what you've done. Perhaps we should think about naming the unit in your honour? I know the board of trustees is trying to decide on a suitable name for the department, and yours seems highly appropriate. The Dominic Walsh Accident and Emergency Clinic—it has a certain ring to it, wouldn't you agree?'

'I don't want thanks or departments named after me,' he snapped. 'That has never been the driving force behind what I do. I want to make a difference to people's lives, Dr Roberts. It's as simple as that.'

'Then the really simple solution is to do what you were trained to do and go back to work.'

She waved a hand towards the crowded waiting room. 'There are plenty of patients who need your skills. I can even offer you a job, at least on a temporary basis until our new registrar is able to take up the post. So what do you say, Dr Walsh? Are you up to the challenge? Or don't I really need to ask you that because I already know what your answer will be?'

She spun round before he could say anything and felt her stomach sink when she realised that they had attracted an audience. Most of the department must have heard what she had said from the stunned expressions on her colleagues' faces. However, it wasn't that which threw her into a complete spin. It was the fact that the whole conversation had apparently been broadcast live on national television!

Michelle pushed her way past the cameraman and hurried to the washroom. She slammed the door and took a deep breath, but she could feel herself trembling as reaction set in. The thought that she had just made a public spectacle of herself was more than she could bear.

She couldn't begin to imagine what the hospital's trustees would say once they found out—if they hadn't already seen the broadcast, of course, and most of the country probably had. There had been advertisements for that week's episode of *Health Matters* in all the papers and they would have drummed up a huge audience. People the length and breadth of Britain had probably sat in their living rooms listening to her telling Dominic Walsh exactly what she thought of him!

Michelle closed her eyes in dismay. What had she done?

'No! Did you hear me, Hugh? N-O—No!'

Dominic swung round and glared at the other man. They were in the trailer again. It was a little after nine p.m., just an hour since Michelle Roberts had seen fit to insult him on national television. Frankly, he still wasn't sure that he could trust himself not to wring her pretty little neck if he bumped into her, which was why he had made a hasty exit after the broadcast had ended. Now it seemed that her outburst was about to have even more repercussions unless he made his position perfectly clear.

'It's out of the question. There's no way that I'll agree.'

'But the phones haven't stopped ringing for the past hour! We've logged over six thousand calls and they're still coming in.' Hugh stared mournfully at him. 'The ratings would go through the roof and you won't even consider the idea?'

'No, I won't! I refuse to let that woman *blackmail* me into working with her.'

Dominic turned to stare out of the window again, afraid of what might be written on his face at that moment. Oh, he was very angry—as he had every right to be—but he was also hurt. Michelle's refusal to believe that he was motivated by a genuine desire to help people had wounded him deeply, but he didn't want Hugh to know that.

'It was more of a *challenge* than an attempt to blackmail you, Dominic,' Hugh said swiftly. 'Surely you don't want folk to think that you're afraid you wouldn't be able to handle it?'

'Stop it, Hugh. You're not going to get me to do what you want by applying a little amateur psychology.' He glanced round and saw Hugh shrug.

'It was worth a try. This could become the hottest show on television if you would only agree to do as Dr Roberts suggested. The audience would be switching on in droves because it's just what triggers the public's interest.'

'What is? Watching me and Michelle Roberts hurling insults at each other?'

'Watching the *sparks* flying between you and the beautiful Dr Roberts,' Hugh corrected.

He held up his hands placatingly when Dominic swore. 'I know, I know. There's nothing going on between you two, but try telling the audience that. Most of the callers have said the same thing—that they sensed there was something more to that argument you two had, something a little more *personal*. It's whetted their appetites and they can't wait to see what's going to happen.'

'You'll be asking me when we're naming the day next.' Dominic snorted in disgust. 'Now, that would really hike up the ratings, wouldn't it? True love blossoms on national television, and the proof is watching me and the beautiful Dr Roberts swearing undying devotion to each other.'

He turned to stare out of the window again, wondering why the thought didn't make him feel as angry as it should have done. There was nothing going on between him and Michelle, but he had to admit that he wouldn't have been averse to a little romance if the situation had been different. He might not have appreciated what she'd said to him, but he didn't deny that she was very attractive. It had been a long time since he'd met a woman who had created such an impression on him.

'Of course not! What do you take me for, Dominic? I don't want you doing anything you aren't happy with.'

'But you still think I should accept her challenge to work at St Justin's for the next month? OK, convince me. There has to be something in it for me, and not just an increase in ratings either.'

He went and sat down. As he swung his feet onto the desk, he found himself thinking wryly that he could never have imagined he would be having this conversation twelve hours ago. He had been more concerned about not causing too many disruptions in the A and E department back then rather than dealing with the crazy ramblings of some overworked medic.

He sighed as that thought struck him. It didn't help to know that Michelle had been working such long hours that day. If he was tired then how much worse must she be feeling? He had seen the hordes of people who had turned up that day and knew how pushed the staff had been to keep on top of things.

From what he had gathered, there were still a number of posts in the department waiting to be filled. Although the facilities had been upgraded, it wasn't worth a brass farthing if there weren't enough staff to do the work.

'Name your price, Dominic. You tell me what you want and I'll get onto our sponsors.' Hugh was beaming, obviously believing that he had made a breakthrough. 'You're due for a salary review in six months' time, but we can bring it forward, probably demand double your original fee.'

'I'm perfectly happy with what I get,' he said impatiently. 'It will take more than a salary increase to make me agree to this crazy plan.'

'OK, so how about some more equipment for the unit? Or backing for another of your pet projects? I'm telling you, Dominic, the sky's the limit on this one.'

The sky's the limit...

He frowned when he heard that. He knew that Hugh hadn't been exaggerating either. Maybe he was being a fool to overlook the possibilities on offer here?

'Is that a fact?' Dominic tilted back his chair and grinned at the other man. 'Give me ten minutes to think about this, Hugh. I might be able to come up with something that makes us both happy. I just want to be sure that I know what I'm doing.'

'When haven't you known *exactly* what you're doing?' Hugh said wryly, standing up. He glanced round when there was a knock on the door. 'It's probably someone after your autograph. Don't worry, I'll get rid of them.'

'Uh-huh.' Dominic didn't bother looking round as Hugh went to the door. He had a plan forming but he wanted to be a hundred per cent certain that it wouldn't backfire on him...

'I'm sorry to bother you, Dr Walsh, but may I have a word with you, please?'

Dominic felt a jolt of ice-cold shock rocket through him when he recognised Michelle Roberts's cool tones. He swung his feet to the floor and stood up, feeling his heart drumming inside his chest when he saw her standing in the doorway.

She had shed her white coat and her slender figure looked strangely ethereal backlit by the glow from the hospital's security lights. She looked so small and defenceless that he found it difficult to equate the woman standing before him with the one who had fired off that salvo of insults an hour earlier.

It made him wonder all of a sudden which was the real Michelle Roberts. Was it the determined professional who had stood up to him with such spirit? Or was it this woman who had an air of vulnerability about her that touched him deeply?

In his heart he knew that he could be making a big mistake, but all of a sudden he knew that he wouldn't rest until he had found out which one was the *real* Michelle Roberts.

*   *   *

Michelle took a deep breath as Dominic continued to stare at her. She wouldn't have blamed him if he ordered her out of the trailer, but at the very least she had to make an attempt to apologise. She had been unforgivably rude tonight and, although she had meant every word, it had been reprehensible to have said what she had in front of countless witnesses.

'I understand how you feel, Dr Walsh,' she began, then stopped when he laughed softly.

'Do you really?'

'Why, yes, of course.' She looked at him in surprise when she heard the wry note in his voice. It was rather dark in the trailer and he was standing with his back to the light so that it was hard to tell what he was thinking. However, he didn't give the appearance of being angry, strangely enough.

She brushed aside that thought, realising how foolish it would be to lower her guard while she was on enemy territory. 'I was very rude to you earlier and although, naturally, I don't retract what I said, I feel that I should apologise if I caused you any embarrassment professionally.'

'Why would you imagine that I'm embarrassed, professionally or otherwise?'

Michelle felt a little ripple of anger fizz along her veins when she heard the amusement in his voice. It was an effort not to let her feelings show. 'Because it wouldn't have enhanced the image you try to project, Dr Walsh. Your adoring public might start wondering why you left medicine to work in television, and they might decide that your reasons were rather less altruistic that they had thought them to be.'

'So our little contretemps might have done a great deal of harm both to me and the programme?'

He rested his hip against the edge of the desk as he regarded her with hooded green eyes. 'Is that why you went on the attack, Michelle? Because you wanted to damage me and my programme?'

'Of course not! What do you take me for?' she denied hotly.

'I don't know you well enough to make snap judgements about your character. Just as you don't know me, but that didn't stop you going for the jugular, did it? Maybe you should have stopped and tried to find out if you were right before you decided to destroy my reputation in front of half the country.'

She winced at that. 'I didn't mean to do that. And I'm more than willing to make a public apology if that's what you want me to do.'

'I haven't yet decided what I want. I'm still trying to make up my mind.'

He smiled thinly and she felt a ripple of alarm run through her as she wondered what he meant. Just for a moment she considered asking him to explain, then she thought better of it. She had done her bit and apologised and now it was up to him to decide if he was prepared to accept it. She certainly didn't intend to *beg* his forgiveness, if that was what he was hoping for!

The thought stiffened her spine and she smiled coolly at him. 'Well, when you do finally make up your mind, you know where to find me. Goodnight, Dr Walsh.'

He didn't try to detain her when she left. He didn't say a word, in fact, although she knew that it wouldn't be the end of the affair. Dominic was choosing his moment to tell her what punishment he intended to extract from her.

It was a highly unsettling thought and she was glad that she had no time to dwell on it when her beeper

sounded. She hurried back to A and E and made straight
for Resus.

'Right, what have we got?' she demanded, dragging
on gloves as she elbowed open the door.

'Michael Derbyshire, adult male with a penetrating
stab wound to the lower right thorax,' John reported,
looking a little green around the gills. It was his first
major incident and Michelle knew how daunting he must
have found it to have to take charge when she hadn't
been around.

'BP and vital signs?' she asked briskly so that he
would have to focus on the job rather than his nerves.

She smiled to herself when he immediately trotted out
the information she had asked for, and she saw Helen
wink at her. Although everyone would deny it with their
last breath, it was an unspoken rule that the newly qualified were treated tenderly. The last thing anyone wanted
to do was scare them off!

'That's great, John. Now, if you wouldn't mind giving
the surgical registrar a call and letting him know that
we'll be sending him a customer, please... Thanks.'

She turned to the patient as the young houseman hurried away. Michael Derbyshire was conscious, although
obviously in pain. There was an inch-wide wound just
below his rib cage and although it wasn't bleeding
heavily, that wasn't an indication of its severity. A single
knife wound like that could inflict a lot of damage to the
underlying tissue.

'Hi, there, I'm Michelle Roberts, the senior registrar.
Can you tell me what happened?' she asked, gently examining the wound.

'I was coming out of the pub and didn't see him,' the
man explained. 'I thought he'd punched me at first until
I saw the blood...' He groaned as she gently removed

some clothing fibres from the wound. 'It doesn't half hurt, Doc!'

'I'm sure it does. I'm going to give you something for the pain, Michael, then send you straight up to the operating theatre. There's not a lot we can do here, to be honest. We'll need to know how much tissue damage you've suffered before we decide how best to treat you,' she told him.

'You mean I'll need an operation and they'll stitch me up?'

'You'll definitely need a thoracotomy—that's an operation to explore inside the chest cavity to see if there's any damage to the vital organs—but the surgeon might decide not to stitch up the wound straight away. Usually it's best if it's left for a few days to make sure that there's no infection.'

'Does that mean I'll have to stay in hospital?' he asked.

'I'm afraid so. Is there anyone you want us to contact for you—wife, mother, sister, brother?'

'Sally, but I don't think you'd better phone her.' Michael grimaced. 'It was her old man who did this to me.'

'I see. Better leave well alone, then.'

Michelle rolled her eyes when Helen grinned at her. If she lived to be a hundred she would never understand how people willingly got into such messes in their relationships.

She sighed as she finished telling Helen which drugs she wanted. It wasn't a problem she would ever have to face, thankfully. She hadn't had a relationship with a man since Stephen had died and didn't intend to. It would be like a betrayal of everything they had meant to one another. Maybe she did get lonely at times, but she had her work and her memories and they were more than enough to fill her life.

It was only as she was drawing up the recommended dose of analgesic that she found herself wondering if they weren't a poor substitute for what she had once dreamed of having. She had always thought that she would have had a family by the time she reached thirty, but she was thirty-three this year, and there was no likelihood of that ever happening. She needed a husband before she had children, and there was nobody in the world who could make her feel like Stephen had.

Unbidden, a picture of Dominic Walsh's handsome face sprang to mind and she flushed. He certainly wasn't husband material even if she'd been in the market for one. Men like Dominic Walsh didn't interest her!

They sent Michael Derbyshire up to Theatre a short time later. It was the end of her shift so Michelle accompanied him as the porter wheeled him to the lift. She only needed to collect her jacket and she would be ready to leave so she had time to spare to reassure him.

'Everything will be fine, Michael. The surgeon will soon sort you out.'

'Thanks, Doc. I really appreciate all you've done for me.' He managed a smile. 'I was a bit worried when I realised it was you. I thought you might give me a tongue-bashing as well.'

'I'm sorry?' she said, frowning.

'I saw you laying into Dominic Walsh on the telly while I was in the pub,' he explained, then suddenly grinned as he looked past her. 'Oh, don't tell me I've got a ringside seat for round two?'

Michelle looked round and flushed when she saw Dominic heading their way. There were still a number of people in the waiting room and she could see everyone turning to look at what was happening. One of the cameramen was hurrying after Dominic, with the sound-recordist tagging on behind.

She swallowed hard but there was a lump the size of Vesuvius in her throat when Dominic stopped in front of her. It had been one thing to offer to apologise to him on live television but quite another to actually have to do it! The thought that people might believe she was backing down was more than she could bear, but there was little she could do about it.

'Dr Roberts, I'm glad I caught you before you left.' He smiled at her but she could see the gleam in his eyes and her worst suspicions were immediately confirmed. Dominic intended to stand there and enjoy watching her eat a large slice of humble pie.

'Dr Walsh.' It was a struggle to get his name out but she'd be damned if she would let him see how uncomfortable she felt. She squared her shoulders and looked him straight in the eye. 'I believe I promised you an apology.'

'I believe you did,' he put in smoothly before she could continue. 'However, that really wasn't what I wanted to talk to you about.'

'It wasn't?' Michelle blinked in surprise. She could hear the camera whirring as their conversation was filmed, but there was nothing she could do about it.

'No.' Dominic treated her to his most charming smile. 'You set me a challenge earlier, Dr Roberts, so I thought I'd give you my answer.'

'Challenge?' she repeated uncertainly.

'Surely you remember?' he said silkily. 'You told me that you could offer me a job here for the next month if I thought I could handle it. Well, I'm sure you'll be happy to learn that I've decided to accept.'

He turned and smiled at the camera. 'From eight o'clock tomorrow morning I shall be a member of Dr Roberts's team, here at St Justin's hospital. Make a note in your diaries, folks, to switch on to *Health Matters* next week and see how I've got on.'

CHAPTER THREE

'CUT! That's it, everyone. We're off the air.'

Dominic relaxed as soon as the red light on the camera went out. He looked round as Hugh came over and clapped him on the shoulder.

'Brilliant! Absolutely first rate, Dominic. You won't regret this, believe me.'

'I hope not.' Dominic smiled but he was very much aware that Michelle hadn't said a word.

He glanced at her and felt a moment's contrition when he saw how pale she looked. Maybe he should have warned her in advance about what he was planning, but he simply hadn't had the time. He had only managed to get everything sorted out to his satisfaction a few minutes before they'd been due to go on air, but there was no way that he could have gone ahead with this if he hadn't covered all the bases.

'Excuse me.'

He jumped when she brushed past him, his hand instinctively going out to detain her as she tried to hurry away. He could tell that she was upset and knew that he had to explain what he was doing.

'Wait a minute, Michelle, I just want to—'

'Want to what? Explain why you decided to set me up like that?' She laughed harshly and he felt his guts twist when he heard the pain in her voice. 'I think it's perfectly clear why you did it, Dr Walsh. Now, if you don't mind, I want to go home. Suffice it to say that this hasn't been the best day I've ever had.'

She stalked past him, her head held so high that it was a wonder she could see where she was going. Dominic felt a rush of impatience at her stubbornness. The wretched woman was determined to see him in the worst possible light but somehow, some *way*, he had to make her understand that she was wrong about him. And he may as well start now!

He strode after her, ignoring the interested looks that followed him as he made his way to the staffroom and thrust open the door. There was no sign of her in there, or in the locker room when he went to check. He went outside and frowned when he spotted her walking up the drive.

She didn't have on a coat or a jacket, just the blouse and skirt she'd been wearing all day. Although it wasn't particularly cold that night, there was a hint of rain in the air. Surely she wasn't going to walk all the way home dressed like that rather than run the risk of having to speak to him?

He sighed heavily as she disappeared through the gates. Oh, yes, she was! He couldn't believe that anyone would be so obstinate, but it went against the grain to know that he was responsible and not do something about it.

He ran to fetch his car and drove swiftly out of the hospital. She was walking at such a pace that she had gone some distance before he caught up with her. Rolling down the car window, he leaned across the passenger seat.

'Get in and I'll run you home.'

'Go away.'

She didn't glance at him or slacken her pace and he felt his irritation move another notch up the scale. Accelerating, he drove on ahead a little way and parked then got out and stood squarely in the middle of the pavement so that he was blocking her path.

'This is ridiculous, Michelle,' he snapped. 'I just want to talk to you and explain why I decided to accept your offer.'

'And I don't want to hear what you have to say so that makes us quits.'

She smiled thinly, her beautiful grey eyes filled with contempt. However, Dominic could see the hurt they held as well and he felt even more wretched because the last thing he'd intended had been to hurt her like that.

'Michelle, I—'

'No, don't bother. If you're going to tell me that it's all arranged and there's nothing I can do about it, there's no point. I know you wouldn't have been rash enough to go on live television and announce that you would be taking the job if you hadn't cleared it with everyone concerned. Am I right, Dr Walsh?'

Her tone cut him to the quick. Maybe he should have felt annoyed by her refusal to listen to him, but it was hard to ignore the wobble in her voice that told him how hard she was finding it to deal with this situation.

'Yes, you're right. The chief executive of St Justin's happens to be a personal friend. He was more than happy about the idea and promised to clear it with the board of trustees.'

He shrugged but it had been a long time since he'd felt as though he'd done something that had lowered his standing in the eyes of someone whose opinion he valued.

He felt a little shock of surprise as that thought sank home, and missed what she said in reply. 'I'm sorry, what was that?'

'I said that I supposed you've cleared it with the local

health authority as well. Or doesn't your influence extend to having friends there as well?'

'I play squash with the director,' he stated shortly, trying to reconcile himself to the idea that he cared what this woman thought of him. Frankly, he found it hard to accept, but he knew in his heart that it was true.

He took a deep breath and forced himself to concentrate on the here and now, not all the funny thoughts that seemed to be invading his head. 'I'm godfather to his granddaughter, as it happens. And I know his wife. She's on the boards of several charities that I support.'

'How cosy. It must be marvellous to have so many friends in such high places.' She stared back at him and her expression was colder than ever. 'You've thought of everything, Dr Walsh, so what do you want from me? My blessing? Sorry, but I'm afraid I can't give you that.'

She tried to step around him but he caught hold of her wrist. 'Can't or won't, Michelle?'

His fingers fastened tighter when she tried to pull away and he was surprised by how fragile the bones in her wrist felt. She was so feisty and determined that it was easy to overlook how small she actually was. The top of her head barely came up to the level of his chin yet she stood so straight that she gave the impression of being much taller.

He felt an unexpected rush of awareness as he began to notice other details as well, like how smooth her skin felt and how fast the pulse in her wrist was racing. He couldn't help wondering what it would be like to feel that wild little rhythm beating away in the hollow of her neck. How sensual it would be to press his mouth to that pulse point and feel her life force beating inside her...

'Both.' She snatched her arm away and glared at him. 'This might be a game to you, but we're dealing with people's lives here. They're entitled to the very best care possible when they come to St Justin's.'

'I agree.' It was an effort to rid himself of such disturbing thoughts but the implied criticism acted like a dousing of cold water. 'And I assure you that I won't be putting anyone's life at risk. I've made a point of keeping up to date with the latest advances in trauma care. I go on a refresher course every six months specifically to do that.'

'Oh, I see.'

She bit her lip and he saw a hint of uncertainty flicker in her eyes. It was only a glimpse but enough to make him wonder if he might be making some headway. He decided that he needed to press home his advantage while he had the chance.

'I don't think you do—see, I mean. I think we need to talk this through without shouting at each other and hurling insults.'

He glanced up as the first spots of rain started to fall and shrugged.

'Why not let me drive you home? If nothing else, it will save you from a soaking.'

She looked up at the sky and sighed. 'I forgot to fetch my jacket from my locker.'

'I know. You were too angry with me, weren't you?'

He smiled at her, praying that she would unbend enough to at least listen to what he had to say even if she refused to believe it. 'How about we call a half-hour truce while I run you home? Maybe we could extend it long enough so that we can talk through your concerns.'

'I'm not about to change my mind, Dominic,' she shot back.

'I know that. And I don't expect you to.'

It was funny how much it had cheered him to hear

her calling him by his first name at last. Maybe it was silly to see it as a good sign but he couldn't help it. If he could just explain what his reasons were for taking the job then surely she would start to understand that he wasn't quite the low-life she thought him to be.

'I just want to put my side of the story to you,' he said quietly, knowing instinctively that it would be best not to put too much pressure on her. 'That's all.'

She hesitated and he saw myriad expressions cross her beautiful face before she suddenly nodded. 'All right, then.'

She walked to the car and opened the door. Dominic let out his breath in a deep sigh as he watched her slide into the seat. At least she had agreed to listen to him. It wasn't much of a victory but it felt as though he had just won a major battle, funnily enough. Now it remained to be seen how much good it would do him.

By the time they drew up outside her flat, Michelle was a bag of nerves. To give Dominic his due he hadn't said anything to upset her on the short drive from the hospital. He had kept the conversation mainly to trivialities like the weather. However, it would have been a massive understatement to say that she was starting to regret caving in.

She turned to him as he switched off the engine, knowing that it was important that she take charge from there on. 'Would you like to come up to my flat? There doesn't seem much point in us sitting here in the car.'

'If you're sure you don't mind,' he replied politely, sliding the keys out of the ignition.

'Of course I don't mind, otherwise I wouldn't have suggested it,' she replied, then bit her lip when she heard the snap in her voice.

She got out of the car and hurried up the front steps then groaned when she realised that she didn't have her keys with her. They were in her bag and her bag was in her locker along with her jacket. Oh, hell!

She pressed the buzzer for the flat next to hers, praying that Carmen wouldn't have gone out. Her friend led an active social life between her bingo sessions and the local church's senior citizen's club, and spent few evenings at home.

'Have you lived here for very long?'

She glanced round when she heard the surprise in Dominic's voice as he took stock of the house's shabby exterior. It was a typical Victorian terraced house and urgently in need of attention. Most of the paint had peeled off the front door and one of the ground-floor windows had been boarded up to stop anyone breaking in after the previous tenant had left. Once upon a time the house would have been owned by a prosperous family, but this part of London was no longer fashionable, and it showed in the state of the run-down property that lined the street.

Living there suited her needs, though, because it was close enough to the hospital to mean that she didn't have to rely on public transport to get to work, and its undesirable location meant that the rent was reasonable enough that she didn't need to share the flat with anyone. However, she could tell at once that he wasn't impressed.

'Four years,' she replied shortly, feeling a little vexed that he had seen fit to criticise. It had nothing to do with him where she chose to live so he could keep his opinions to himself.

She turned her back on him when she heard Carmen's voice coming through the intercom speaker. 'Carmen, it's me, Michelle. I've forgotten my keys. Can you let me in?'

She pushed open the door as soon as the lock was released and led the way inside. 'I'm on the third floor—Oh, watch out for the top stair, by the way. One of the boards is loose and I wouldn't want you to trip over it.'

She didn't check to see if he'd heeded her warning as she hurried up the flights of stairs. Carmen came to her door when she heard their footsteps on the landing and smiled in delight when she saw Dominic.

'Ah, I see you have company tonight, darling. Good, good. It's about time you thought about something other than sick people.' She treated Dominic to her most winsome smile as she held out a vermilion-tipped hand. 'Carmen Rivera. I'm Michelle's dearest friend. She must have told you about me?'

'It's a pleasure to meet you, Miss Rivera.'

Michelle hid a smile as she watched Dominic shaking the woman's hand. Carmen was dressed in one of her more understated outfits that night, but it was a startling creation by most people's standards. Gold Lurex and marabou feathers, dressed down by the addition of the latest in high-tech trainers, wasn't the normal attire people would expect an octogenarian to wear, but to give Dominic his due he didn't bat an eyelid.

'I have a feeling that we have met before,' Carmen declared, holding onto his hand. 'Your grandfather doesn't attend the socials at St Giles's, does he?'

'I'm afraid not.'

He treated Carmen to a warm smile and Michelle was surprised by how genuine it appeared to be. She would have expected him to be a little put out by the fact that the old lady hadn't recognised him from his television show, but it didn't seem to have bothered him. 'And I'm sure I wouldn't have forgotten if we had met before.'

'How nice of you to say so,' Carmen purred. She let go of his hand and winked at Michelle. 'I mustn't keep you. I'm sure you two young people have better things to do with your evening than spend it talking to an old lady.'

Michelle felt herself blush at the less than subtle hint about what Dominic was doing there. 'Dominic and I have some work-related matters to discuss, Carmen.'

'Of course!' the old woman replied airily. She felt in her pocket and handed Michelle a key. 'Don't forget to let me have it back, darling, if you're going to be late home tomorrow. Dulcie's had her supper but she's not in the best of moods, I'm afraid.'

'Oh, great. Just what I need.' Michelle smiled ruefully as she took the key. 'Thanks, Carmen. I'll slip it under your door on my way out in the morning.'

She turned to Dominic as the old lady went back inside her flat. 'Just be careful when we go in. Don't make any sudden moves.'

'Why? Does your flatmate have something against you inviting visitors home?'

She hid her smile when she heard the bewilderment in his voice. 'You could say that.'

She unlocked the door and slid her hand round the jamb to switch on the light. There was no sound from inside the flat, which was always a bad sign.

'Dulcie, it's me,' she called softly, creeping into the hall. She heard Dominic following her and raised a warning hand. 'Maybe you should wait outside while I find out where she is.'

The words were barely out of her mouth when a spitting bundle of fur suddenly hurled itself along the hall, bypassing her and making straight for Dominic. Michelle heard his gasp of pain as sharp feline teeth connected with soft ankle tissue and groaned in dismay.

'Stop that, Dulcie! Let go, you wicked, wicked girl!'

She scooped the hissing cat into her arms and carried her into the living room, keeping tight hold of the animal as she switched on the lamps.

Dominic warily poked his head round the door. 'Is it safe? Or should I wait out here until you've got your guard-cat under control?'

'She should be fine now,' she assured him, keeping a firm hold on the cat's tortoiseshell fur as he inched his way into the room.

'You mean, once she's had her quota of human flesh she's satisfied for the night?' he suggested with a hint of wry amusement in his voice that made her laugh.

'Something like that.'

She groaned when she saw him limping further into the room. 'I really am sorry. I should have made you wait outside until I'd tested the lie of the land.'

'Does she do this often? Take chunks out of your visitors, I mean?' he asked, keeping a wary eye on the cat as he sat on the sofa and rolled down the top of his black sock.

'I don't have that many visitors, which is probably part of the problem,' she explained, putting Dulcie down so that she could take a look at how much damage the cat had caused.

She knelt on the floor in front of the sofa and ran a practised eye over the two tiny puncture marks just above his left ankle-bone. 'If it's any consolation, I think you'll live.'

She ran an exploratory finger over the hair-roughened flesh. 'Have you had a tetanus booster recently?'

'I...um...yes.' He cleared his throat and she looked at him in alarm when she heard the huskiness in his voice.

'Are you sure you're OK? It's probably given you a bit of fright...'

'No, I'm fine,' he said quickly. He summoned a smile but she could see the oddest expression in his green eyes before his lids abruptly lowered. 'Really. There's no need to worry.'

'Oh. Good.' Michelle took a quick breath but for some reason her heart seemed to be racing as she got to her feet. She glanced down as the cat came to her and started to twine itself sinuously around her legs. 'There's no point doing that now, madam. You're not going to get round me that easily. You're a very bad girl.'

Dominic grinned ruefully as he looked at the cat. 'She looks as though butter wouldn't melt in her mouth now. How long have you had her?'

'Two years. I found her in a garbage bin. Someone had put her in a plastic bag and thrown her onto the rubbish.'

She ran a gentle hand over the cat's soft fur, relieved to have something to take her mind off the strange way her heart seemed to be behaving. 'I heard her meowing as I walked past, otherwise she would have been carted off to the dump.'

'Poor little thing. It's incredible how cruel people can be, isn't it?'

Michelle sighed sadly when she heard the disgust in his voice. 'It is. She was a bag of bones when I brought her home and she wouldn't let me go anywhere near her. I used to have to leave her food in a dish then go out of the room before she would eat. It's taken a while to get her to trust me, but she still isn't good with strangers, as you've discovered to your cost.'

She realised that to disguise her nervousness she was talking too much. 'Anyway, I'll go and get some antiseptic to put on that bite. I wouldn't like it to get infected.'

She went to pick up the cat, but Dulcie slipped past her and hid under the sideboard, swishing her tail warningly when Michelle tried to coax her to come out.

'Leave her. I'm sure she won't take a second chunk out of me.' Dominic smiled when she looked uncertainly at him. 'I don't imagine I taste all that good, but I can always call for help if she comes back for seconds.'

She returned his smile, thinking how good he had been about what had happened. A lot of people would have made a fuss if they'd been bitten like that, but he hadn't.

'Well, if you're sure, I won't be long.'

She hurried from the room and went straight to the kitchen, where she switched on the kettle before taking the first-aid box out of the cupboard. The fact that Dominic hadn't reacted as she would have expected him to do puzzled her a bit. It made her wonder if she had been too hasty in summing him up, and that wasn't the most comfortable of thoughts when she needed to keep a clear head.

She made two mugs of instant coffee and put them on a tray, along with a bowl of warm water and the first-aid box. Dominic was still sitting on the sofa and he looked round when she came back into the room.

'I really like what you've done with this room. It looks so…well, *cosy* I suppose is the word I'm looking for.'

'Thank you.' She couldn't deny that she was pleased

by the compliment. 'It took me ages to get the place exactly how I wanted it.'

She smiled as she looked around the room. She had painted the walls a rich, old-gold colour and had chosen the same colour for the curtains that draped the high sash windows. She rarely used the central light fixture, preferring the softer effect gained from the various lamps that she had dotted about, and the whole room seemed to glow in the light from them. Most of the furniture had been bought secondhand from the local flea market, but she had spent hours lovingly polishing the wood until it gleamed and making new wine-coloured covers for the old sofa and armchair.

She was rather surprised that it was to Dominic's taste because nothing she owned was worth much in monetary terms, although it meant a lot to her. However, there wasn't any doubt in her mind that he had told her the truth when she saw the appreciative expression on his face.

It was another unsettling sign that she might have been wrong about him so she drove it from her mind as she put the tray on the table in front of the sofa. 'I've made us some coffee but let me take a look at your ankle first.'

'It's OK. I can do it.'

He treated her to a smile but she couldn't ignore the fact that he had been very quick to refuse her help. Had the thought of her attending to his injury been so distasteful, then?

'Fine.' She took one of the mugs off the tray, trying to clamp down on the ridiculous sense of hurt she felt. So what if he didn't want her help? Why should it matter? Yet she knew in her heart that it did.

She watched in silence as he quickly swabbed his ankle with a damp cotton-wool ball then pulled up his sock. It was on the tip of her tongue to point out that he should really put some antiseptic on it, but she decided that he probably wouldn't welcome her interference. He dropped the cotton wool back onto the tray and smiled at her.

'That should do. Now, to get back to the reason why you invited me up here. I want to make it absolutely clear before we go any further that I'm not trying to pay you back for what happened earlier tonight, Michelle.'

'No?' She didn't bother trying to hide her scepticism and heard him sigh.

'No. Oh, I admit I was furious about what you said to me, but in a way it was my own fault.'

'Your fault?' she said in surprise. 'Why?'

'Because I should have noticed that we were being filmed and put a stop to it.' He shrugged, his broad shoulders rising and falling beneath his expensive jacket. 'It was pure carelessness and I have no excuse.'

'So you didn't know that the cameras were running?' she asked with a frown, wondering if he was telling her the truth.

'I had no idea.' He leant forward and his eyes seemed to blaze as he looked at her. 'It wasn't a set-up, Michelle. I want you to believe that. It isn't the sort of thing I would do, and certainly not to you.'

She shivered when she heard the urgency in his voice. It was obviously important to Dominic that she believe him, but why should it matter so much?

He sighed when she didn't say anything. 'I can tell you aren't convinced so maybe I should cut to the chase and explain what I hope to achieve by working at St Justin's for the next few weeks.'

'That's probably the best idea,' she said as coolly as

she could, but she had to admit that she felt a little bit shaken. She wouldn't have imagined that it would make any difference to him what she thought. He would still go ahead with this plan despite any objections she might make.

The thought steadied her and she smiled cynically. 'Although it doesn't take a genius to work out that you're hoping to increase the number of viewers who watch your programme.'

'Of course. The better the viewing figures the more power it gives me to produce the kind of programmes that I'm aiming for,' he said bluntly. 'If the response we've had today is anything to go by then we're guaranteed to beat all our previous figures. A lot of people watched today's bulletins and they'll switch on again to see what's happening during the next four weeks.'

'So does that mean that we'll have to put up with being filmed every day for the next month? Because if it does then I'm certainly not happy about the idea,' she shot back, stung by the thought that she had allowed herself to be duped into listening when the only interests that would be served by this crazy plan were Dominic's own.

'The plan is to have just one cameraman in the unit, not the whole crew. The same conditions will apply as today, that is, nobody will be filmed without their permission, and that goes for the staff as well as the patients,' he explained. 'There will be minimal disruption and you have my word on that, although I'm not sure if it carries very much weight.'

Michelle flinched when she heard the acerbic note in his voice but she refused to apologise if that was what he was hoping for. 'And what—if anything—will St Justin's get out of all this?'

'For a start, publicity, and before you turn up your nose, consider exactly what it could mean.'

Dominic took a sip of his coffee and regarded her levelly. 'You've had a lot of trouble filling all the staffing vacancies since the refurbishment was completed. You're in desperate need of three more full-time nurses, another senior registrar and a houseman. You've also not found a suitably qualified trauma surgeon so you haven't been able to open your new emergency theatre.'

'You have certainly been doing your homework.'

'Yes, I have.' He put his cup on the tray and leant forward. 'St Justin's A and E department could be the very best of its kind in the whole of Greater London if you had the right staffing levels. Once we go on air each week I can guarantee that you'll have people queueing up to work there. You'll be able to take your pick, Michelle, so tell me that isn't a tempting prospect.'

'Of course it's tempting! Staffing has been our biggest headache. Even some of our former members of staff decided not to take up their old jobs when we were due to reopen. It's not easy working in any A and E department.'

'It isn't. But once people see the true value of the work you do, they'll want to be a part of it.'

'And they are the only reasons why you accepted my challenge—to hike up your ratings and encourage people to apply for our vacant posts?' she said sceptically.

'No, there's a third. If this goes ahead then the show's sponsors have agreed to fund another intensive-care bed for the next two years. They will cover all the equipment costs and the staff's salaries. A lot of the people you treat in A and E need IC beds and they're always at a premium.'

Michelle frowned because she couldn't dispute what

he had said. All too often the deciding factor in a patient's recovery was the after-care they received. Then there was the prospect of having a full complement of staff. It would ease everyone's life, hers included, so did she really have the right to put obstacles in the way?

'All right, then. I'm prepared to co-operate.' She shrugged when he looked at her in surprise. 'If having you there achieves what you've just told me, it will be worth having to put up with a few weeks of inconvenience.'

'You won't regret it, Michelle. I promise you.'

'We'll see.' She stood up, wanting to make it clear that the conversation was over. Suddenly, she knew that she'd had enough for one day. It was a relief when Dominic immediately put his cup on the tray and stood.

'I'd better go. You must be tired after the busy day you've had. By the way, I forgot to ask you earlier what had happened about the baby's mother.' He sighed as he followed her into the hall. 'I didn't get a chance to go and see how she was doing before I left, unfortunately.'

Michelle hid her surprise. It had never occurred to her that he would want to visit the girl. 'She's not too good, I'm afraid. She'd lost a lot of blood and the staff are a bit worried about her.'

'What a shame. Have they found out her name yet?'

'Not yet. The police are checking the missing persons register.'

She reached past him and opened the front door, suddenly eager for him to leave. His concern had sounded genuine and once again she found herself wondering if she had misjudged him.

'I hope I've managed to set your mind at rest, Michelle,' he said softly as he paused. He took hold of her hand and squeezed it gently. 'This is going to work out, really it is.'

'We'll see.' It was an effort to smile when all these uncertainties kept surfacing. Could she really believe that Dominic was the caring kind of individual he was making himself out to be when her every instinct told her differently?

She heard him sigh and froze when he suddenly bent and brushed her cheek with his lips. 'I expect so. Goodnight, Michelle. Thanks for the coffee and for listening to me.'

Michelle closed the door as he turned and walked along the landing. She heard his footsteps going down the stairs and it felt as though her heart was beating in time to them...thud, thud, thud.

She went back to the living room and sank down on the sofa, feeling sick and shaken. Dulcie came and jumped on her lap, purring softly in feline apology for her earlier misdemeanours.

Michelle buried her face in the cat's soft fur, but the tingling sensation in her cheek didn't go away. She could feel the imprint of Dominic's lips like a brand on her skin, and she shivered because the idea scared her so much.

She didn't want Dominic Walsh disrupting her life! She was perfectly happy the way she was. She had a job she loved and which gave a purpose to her days. She didn't want anything to change, certainly didn't want a man like him to make her start wishing for something she could never have. She had sworn to herself when Stephen had died that she would remain faithful to his memory, and she had never been tempted to break that vow...

Until now.

CHAPTER FOUR

'ROAD TRAFFIC ACCIDENT arriving in three minutes. Ten-year-old boy. Paramedics haven't found anything major wrong with him, but they're bringing him in to be checked over.'

Ruth Humphries looked around the staffroom. 'So who wants to forfeit their break this time?'

'My turn.'

Dominic felt a rush of adrenaline hit his system as he stood up. It was the third day of his stint at St Justin's and he had to admit that he was enjoying himself enormously. He had forgotten how good it felt to be at the cutting edge.

He laughed as a chorus of cat-calls greeted his announcement. 'OK, I admit it, I need the practice. But if anyone wants to take over, don't let me stop you.'

'No way, superstar.' Bryan Patterson, a junior registrar, grinned at him. 'You've led a charmed life for the past couple of years and it's about time you got down to some real work for a change.'

'I'd argue with you about that if I had the time,' Dominic shot back, heading for the door.

He grinned as he hurried along the corridor. The staff had been absolutely great, treating him as one of them ever since he'd started. Oh, they teased him unmercifully, of course, but he wouldn't have had it any other way. They seemed to have accepted him completely, with one noticeable exception. He sighed as he rounded the corner and caught sight of Michelle coming out of one of the examination cubicles.

She was still very reserved around him and he wasn't sure what he could do about it. He'd hoped that she might have softened towards him after the talk they'd had, but it hadn't happened. Not for the first time he found himself wishing that he hadn't kissed her the other night.

He still wasn't sure why he'd done it, neither had he been able to put it out of his mind. Frankly, he couldn't believe that one chaste peck on the cheek could have had such a lingering effect, although if he'd had the sense to think about how he'd felt when she'd examined his injured ankle, maybe he wouldn't be in this predicament. Michelle Roberts did strange things to his equilibrium, whether he liked the idea or not!

Dominic shrugged aside that unsettling thought as he went outside to meet the ambulance. One of the crew was the same young woman paramedic he'd met when the baby had been found, and she grinned when she saw him.

'Did you enjoy your stint here so much that you decided to stay a bit longer?'

'Something like that.' He smiled back then turned his attention to the patient as the paramedics lifted the stretcher out of the back of the ambulance. 'Hi, there. I'm Dr Walsh. I believe you've been playing tag with a car and you came off worse.'

'My mum's going to kill me,' the boy muttered. 'I've put a hole in the knee of my new jeans.'

Dominic laughed as he held open the swing doors so that the paramedics could push the trolley inside. 'I'm sure she'll let you off just this once.'

He glanced round as Michelle appeared, wondering

why his heart had given a sudden little jerk, like an engine that had been kick-started to life. It was an effort to appear calm when she came and stood next to him, but not for the world would he let her know how uncomfortable he felt.

'RTA,' he explained smoothly. 'I'm just going to take him through to Resus and check him over.'

'Fine,' she agreed politely.

She turned to the child and Dominic saw her expression soften as she smiled at the boy. Just for a second he was overcome by something that felt almost like jealousy when he saw how natural she was with the child. It was such a marked contrast to the way she behaved around him that he couldn't help feeling put out before he realised how ridiculous he was being.

'Hello, I'm Michelle Roberts, one of the doctors here at St Justin's. Can you tell me your name?'

'Liam Hughes,' the boy told her. He glanced at the young woman paramedic and sighed heavily. 'I already told her my name when we were in the ambulance.'

'Did you?' Michelle smiled calmly at the child. 'Sorry, but we need to know who you are and where you live so that we can get in touch with your parents. Is there anyone at home today?'

Liam tried to shake his head and grimaced when he discovered that he couldn't move it because of the cervical collar the paramedics had fitted. 'No. My mum's at work. My nan should be in, though.'

He tried to prise his fingers under the collar to undo it, but Dominic quickly stepped forward. He knew that there had been another purpose to Michelle's questions other than simply finding out background information. Checking that a patient could answer a few simple questions was an excellent way of assessing his levels of consciousness, always an issue of concern in a situation like this.

'Leave that on for a bit longer, son. We want to make sure that you haven't hurt your neck. OK?'

'S'ppose so,' Liam agreed reluctantly.

'Good lad!' Dominic gave the boy's shoulder an encouraging squeeze then turned to Michelle as the paramedics wheeled the trolley into Resus. He felt a little ripple of surprise run through him when he saw the warmth in her grey eyes. Was that really for him?

It was an effort to disguise how much the thought pleased him, but he wasn't about to make a fool of himself all over again. 'Fancy helping me out here?'

'If you want me to.'

She gave him a quick and wholly impersonal smile and the little bubble of happiness that had formed at the thought that she might be softening towards him popped. Fat chance of that ever happening!

'Right, Liam, we're going to move you onto the bed now.' He cleared his mind of such thoughts as he went over to the child. 'Just relax and we promise not to drop you.'

He glanced up as Michelle and the paramedics took up their positions in readiness to lift the child off the trolley. 'On my count, everyone—one, two, three.'

They quickly transferred the child to the bed. Dominic smiled his thanks as the paramedics moved the trolley out of the way. 'Thanks. Sorry, I still haven't found out your names.'

'I'm Lisa Prentice and this is Si Watson, otherwise known as the "A" team,' the young woman explained with a grin. She was in her mid-twenties with a cap of short, honey-brown curls and a rather endearing gap between her top front teeth.

'I didn't know the paramedics used letters to designate the teams,' he observed, frowning.

'Not officially,' Lisa declared. 'But if you've got it then flaunt it, isn't that right, Si?'

'Yep,' the other paramedic replied laconically. He was a little older than Lisa with thinning blond hair and a friendly smile. 'We named ourselves the ''A'' team because we provide such a first-class service to all our customers.'

He winked and Dominic laughed. 'I'll remember that. Anyway, thanks, guys. See you later, no doubt.'

He turned his attention to the boy as soon as they had left. Amy Carlisle, the young nurse to whom he had spoken on the day of their first broadcast, was cutting off Liam's jeans with a pair of blunt-tipped scissors, much to the child's dismay.

Dominic left her to get on with it while he began his examination. The list of possible injuries resulting from a road traffic accident was endless and he needed to rule them all out before he would be completely happy.

'Where exactly does it hurt, Liam?' he asked, running his hands gently over the child's torso and arms while he checked for fractures.

Liam's collar-bones, ribs and both his arms seemed to be fine so next he flexed the child's fingers, taking care not to touch the abrasions on the boy's palms. Young Liam must have tried to save himself when he had been knocked over, and there was a lot of dirt and gravel embedded in his hands that would need to be removed.

'My knee's sore and my head hurts a bit,' Liam admitted. 'I think I hit it on the kerb when I fell over, but I'm not really sure.'

'What were you doing when the car hit you?' Dominic asked, moving to the top of the bed while he gently felt the boy's skull. Amy had finished removing the boy's jeans and Michelle was examining his knee now. It made it quicker if the two of them worked in tandem like this, although he had to admit to feeling a bit surprised by how smoothly it was all going.

'I got a scooter for my birthday,' the boy muttered. 'I thought I'd have a go while Mum was at work. She won't let me take it out on the road, you see, but it's no fun just using it in the park. She'll go mad when she finds out.'

'I don't expect she'll be too pleased,' Dominic agreed drily. He frowned when he discovered a quite noticeable swelling on the right side of the boy's head. 'You've got a nasty lump here, young man. Does it hurt very much?'

'Ouch! Yes!' Liam's eyes filled with tears all of a sudden. 'Will you get my mum to come? I want her here.'

'One of the reception staff have phoned her,' Michelle said soothingly from the foot of the bed, where she was now examining the boy's lower legs and feet. She glanced at Amy. 'Can you make sure that Lisa or Si passed on the details before they left?'

She turned to Dominic as the young nurse hurried away. 'His knee is badly bruised and there's heavy swelling in the area. I think it needs X-raying in case the patella has been dislocated.'

He nodded. 'And I want a CT scan done as well. I want to make certain that there's been no damage done to his head. That's quite a knock he's had and I don't want to take any chances.'

'Right. Want me to set everything up, or would you prefer to do it yourself?'

He frowned at that. 'It doesn't really matter. You do that while I carry on examining him.'

He saw a little colour touch her cheeks and sighed as she moved away. All this unnecessary politeness was starting to get him down. However, there was little he could do about it if she insisted on behaving like that whenever he was around.

He took an ophthalmoscope off the trolley and smiled at the boy. 'I'm going to check your eyes with the aid of this torch, Liam.' He cupped his hand round the end so that the boy could see the tiny light it gave off.

'I didn't hurt my eyes,' Liam protested. 'I just banged my head and hit my knee. I told you that.'

'I know, but I can tell all sorts of things from looking at your eyes.' Dominic smiled reassuringly because he could tell that the boy was starting to get upset. 'It won't hurt and it only takes a minute. OK?'

'Suppose,' the boy replied grudgingly, but he lay still while Dominic shone the beam of light into each of his eyes in turn.

Dominic frowned as he switched off the torch. Both pupils had reacted as they should, but he couldn't shake off the feeling that there might be something wrong. Still, the CT scan would show up any problems. He looked round as the door opened and Mike Soames, the cameraman, came in.

'Amy just told me that you were in here,' Mike explained. 'I was up in the canteen, having some breakfast. Have I missed much?'

Dominic shook his head. 'I'm not sure...' he began, then stopped when Michelle suddenly appeared.

'There's no way that you can film the child without his mother's permission,' she said firmly. 'Apart from anything else, it might upset him.'

'I agree.' He smiled thinly, feeling both irritated and hurt that she believed he would have taken advantage of the situation that way. 'I was just about to tell Mike that, in fact.'

'Oh. I see.' She looked momentarily unsure before she quickly rallied. 'Anyway, Liam can have both his X-ray and the CT scan done straight away. I'll get a porter to take him along to the radiology unit.'

'Fine.'

Dominic turned to Mike as she moved away. Frankly, it surprised him that he let her get to him that way. He knew how she felt about him so why didn't he simply accept it and ignore her? However, he knew in his heart that ignoring Michelle was the one thing he couldn't do, and it bothered him. Exactly what kind of a hold did Michelle Roberts have over him?

'I'll give you a call when the boy's mother arrives. If she says it's all right, we can include a report about this on next week's programme.'

It was an effort to focus on what needed doing but he made himself put all thoughts of Michelle and the effect she had on him out of his head. He had a job to do— *two* jobs, in fact—and he owed it to everyone concerned to do them to the very best of his ability.

'The boy got run over by a car while he was using one of those new scooters that are all the rage at the moment. It will be a warning for other youngsters and their parents to take more care.'

'Fine by me,' Mike agreed easily. 'I'll go outside and pester Amy instead. Oh, what a hard life this is!'

Dominic laughed softly as the cameraman hurried away. If he wasn't mistaken there might be a hint of romance in the air!

He turned as he heard Michelle talking to Liam and frowned. Did Michelle have anyone special in her life? he suddenly wondered. She seemed so self-contained that it was hard to imagine her sharing all the day-to-day intimacies that went with a relationship. Although she was obviously highly thought of by the rest of the staff, he didn't get the impression that she had any really close friends in the department.

Of course, it could be that she preferred not to mix with the people she worked with in her free time, but he didn't think it was that. It was as though she had erected an invisible barrier around herself and kept everyone at arm's length.

Or maybe the real explanation was that she had put up the barrier specifically to keep him away. After all, he had no way of knowing how she acted when he wasn't around.

It was funny how hurtful he found that thought.

Michelle shot a wary glance over her shoulder and let out a sigh of relief when she saw Dominic turn away. She had been conscious of him watching her while she'd been speaking to Liam and it was a relief when she realised that she was no longer the object of his interest.

She had tried her best to deal with the situation, but she still hadn't got used to having him around all the time. She found herself having to steel herself each time they spoke because she was so afraid that she would give herself away.

Dominic disturbed her. He made her feel things she didn't want to feel. He had the power to turn her life upside down but she wouldn't let that happen. She couldn't live with herself if she betrayed Stephen's memory.

'The porter's here. Shall we get Liam through to Radiology?'

She jumped when Dominic came up behind her, feeling her heart starting to race when she swung round. Just for a second her eyes met his and she saw the growing concern they held.

'Is everything all right, Michelle?'

'Fine. Why shouldn't it be?'

She brushed past him and went to speak to the porter, terrified that he might try to question her again. The thought that he might realise how vulnerable she was around him scared her stiff.

'Can you take the patient to Radiology, please? They're expecting him, but tell them I'll be along shortly.'

'I'll go. He is my patient, Michelle. Or don't you trust me enough to take responsibility for him?'

She frowned when she heard the biting note in Dominic's voice. She waited until the porter had wheeled Liam from the room before she replied. 'I don't know what you mean.'

'No?' He folded his arms and regarded her thoughtfully. 'So you've had a complete change of heart since I started working here? I got the distinct impression a few days ago that you didn't believe I could handle the job.'

'You're mistaken, Dr Walsh. It wasn't your ability that I questioned but your motives, if you recall.'

She shrugged but it was hard to feign an indifference she didn't feel. Although Dominic had shed his designer clothes in favour of something more suitable for the job he was now doing, he still presented an imposing figure.

He was wearing black trousers and a black shirt that day, and the colour simply enhanced his dark good looks. His skin was lightly tanned, his black hair perfectly groomed, the faint tang of some kind of expensive cologne just strong enough to make itself noticeable without being cloying. Michelle knew that she would be lying if she claimed that she wasn't aware of him, and didn't try. She had to be honest with herself and see him as the threat he was, not try to pretend.

'Ah, yes, my motives, the motives we discussed at some length the other night in your flat.' He smiled thinly, his green eyes glittering with something that looked more like hurt than anger, funnily enough.

The realisation surprised her so much that she missed what he said and looked at him with bewildered grey eyes. 'What did you say?'

'That I apologise for kissing you the other night. If I'd had any idea that it would cause all these problems, I would never have given in to the impulse.'

So that was what it had been? she thought. An impulse. It should have been a comfort to hear that but it left her feeling oddly dissatisfied.

She brushed aside that foolish thought and looked him straight in the eye. 'It hasn't caused any problems, I assure you. Now, I think one of us has a patient waiting.'

'Of course. And I'm pleased to hear that I haven't blotted my copybook, Michelle.' He treated her to a last, cool smile then left the room.

Michelle followed him out to the corridor, frowning as she watched him walking swiftly towards the new radiology unit. She wasn't sure why he had seen fit to mention what had happened the other night. Nothing that had been said earlier had led up to it. Had it been preying on his mind perhaps?

The thought that Dominic might have found it as difficult as she had to dismiss the memory of that kiss wasn't comforting. It stayed at the back of her mind for the rest of the morning, springing up at any unwary moment until she could cheerfully have screamed. It was a relief when it was time for her lunch-break because it had been such an effort to keep her mind on the job.

She went to the canteen, hoping that she wouldn't run into Dominic in there. She hadn't seen him since he had gone to the radiology unit and wasn't sure which lunch he was on. Because he was working as an extra member of staff he was free to come and go when he chose, although he had been very good about fitting in with the needs of the department. In fact, he had been an asset rather than a liability, as she had feared he would be. He was friendly with the staff, good with the patients and she couldn't fault his work.

Michelle sighed as she plonked a plate of ham sandwiches onto her tray. At this rate she'd soon be a paid-up member of the wretched man's fan club!

Ruth Humphries was just finishing her lunch and she waved when she saw Michelle looking for somewhere to sit. 'Here you are. I'll be going in a minute so you can have the table all to yourself and enjoy a bit of peace and quiet.'

'Do I look that harassed?' Michelle asked ruefully, sitting down.

'I've seen you looking better,' Ruth replied cheerfully. 'What's up?'

'How about too much work and too little time to do it?' she suggested, peeling the plastic film off her sandwich.

'Nothing new there, then.' Ruth laughed. 'And to think I naïvely believed that having all this brand spanking new equipment would mean an end to all the stress. Still, kidding aside, it has been better, don't you think?'

'Oh, yes, of course it has,' she said quickly, feeling guilty. 'Take no notice of me. I don't know why I'm in such a gloomy mood.'

'It's not got anything to do with Dominic, has it?' Ruth suggested. 'I get the impression that you still aren't happy about him being around, but you have to admit that he's been a big help.'

'Of course he has. And, no, I'm not trying to deny it.' She pulled the crust off her sandwich and stared at it.

'But? I sense there was a but in there, Michelle, so what's bothering you? Is it the thought of being on television that you don't like?'

'Probably,' she said quickly, not wanting the other woman to start digging any deeper. Although Ruth meant well there was no way that she could share her concerns with her when it would mean admitting why Dominic disturbed her so much.

She had never discussed her past with her colleagues, preferring to keep that part of her life completely private. She knew how fast gossip spread around a hospital and hated the thought of people talking about her. It was one of the reasons why she had been so wary about making friends with the people she worked with.

Friendship came with strings attached; people expected you to open up to them. The thought of having to tell anyone about Stephen's tragic death had been more than she could face when she'd started work at St Justin's. As the years had passed it had become increasingly difficult to talk about it when people would have wondered why she had kept it secret for such a long time.

Now she fixed a bright smile to her face, hoping that it would allay Ruth's suspicions. 'I don't like to think that I'll look like a complete idiot when the programme is on air.'

'Rubbish! There's no way that you'll come across as anything other than what you are—a caring and dedicated doctor.' Ruth suddenly smiled. 'Here's Dominic now so why don't you tell him about your concerns? I'm sure he'll be able to put your mind at rest.'

Michelle glanced over her shoulder and felt her heart sink when she saw him heading in their direction. 'I'd rather not mention it to him, actually, Ruth,' she said hurriedly.

'Fair enough. It's up to you, of course.' Ruth didn't say anything more because Dominic had reached their table by that point. She got up and grinned at him. 'I've kept your chair warm for you.'

'Thanks.' Dominic treated her to a smile before he looked enquiringly at Michelle. 'Mind if I join you?'

She shrugged, knowing that it would be silly to make an issue out of it. 'Of course not.'

She searched for something to say as Ruth left and Dominic began unloading his tray. The thought of being forced to eat her lunch with him was making her feel very edgy but she couldn't bear to let him see how she felt. 'How was Liam's CT scan?'

'There was a small area of extradural bleeding where he hit his head. I got onto the neurosurgical registrar and he should be going up to Theatre any moment. His mum's arrived, so that's good, and everyone is pretty confident that there won't be any problems about stopping the bleed. Basically, it's fingers crossed, but he should be all right.'

He twisted the cap off his bottle of sparkling mineral water and grimaced as a spray of water shot out of the top, drenching them both. 'Oops, sorry about that. Here.' He passed Michelle a paper napkin to dry herself off.

'Thanks.'

She patted herself dry then handed back the napkin so that he could use it, freezing when he leant over the table and carefully blotted some moisture off the edge of her jaw.

'You missed a bit,' he explained quietly, but she heard the sudden huskiness in his voice and her heart started to race. When he reached for the bottle of water again she visibly jumped and heard him sigh.

'Is it just me who has this effect on you, Michelle? I keep telling myself that it's crazy to think that, but I've seen how you react with the patients and you're absolutely fine with them. I know we got off to a bad start but we'll never sort this out if you don't try to relax when I'm around.'

'I've no idea what you're talking about,' she denied, feeling the hot colour flooding her face. She went to push back her chair but was forced to stop when someone walked past their table.

'Of course you have. You're as jumpy as a kitten around me so I just want to know what I've done. Frankly, I'm finding it very difficult to understand why you're so on edge all the time.'

Dominic's green eyes seemed to burn as he leant towards her. 'Talk to me, Michelle. Tell me what's wrong and what I can do to make it right between us. I'm willing to do anything and everything I can to make your life easier for the next few weeks while I'm here.'

There was no doubting his sincerity and Michelle felt a lump come to her throat. It was so long since anyone had cared about her feelings this way that she didn't know how to handle the situation.

She shot to her feet, uncaring that she nearly cannoned into the people behind her. She heard Dominic call her name but she didn't look at him as she scooped up her tray and hurried across the canteen.

It took only seconds to stack it on the trolley and then

she was heading for the door. She glanced back over her shoulder, wondering frantically if he would follow her, wondering what she would say if he did, but he was sitting exactly where she had left him. In that moment she knew that he wouldn't try again to make her accept him. As far as Dominic was concerned, he had done everything he could and now it was up to her to make the next move.

She bit her lip as she hurried from the canteen, feeling the foolish tears burning her eyes because she knew that it wasn't going to happen. She couldn't make friends with Dominic Walsh because she knew in her heart that friendship would never be enough.

CHAPTER FIVE

DOMINIC soon discovered that his appetite had disappeared. He took his tray back to the counter and placed it on the trolley then left the canteen.

He made his way to the lift but paused when he realised that he couldn't face seeing Michelle again so soon. He needed to think about what had happened and try to get it into perspective before he saw her again. At the moment, he wasn't sure that he would be able to hide how much it had hurt him to watch her running off like that.

His mouth thinned as he recalled the fear he had seen in her eyes. It wasn't easy to accept that she was afraid of him, but what else could he think? He longed to make her tell him what he had done, but he knew in his heart that it would be a mistake to try and press her. He certainly didn't want to risk making a bad situation worse!

Dominic sighed as he opened the fire-door and ran lightly down the stairs. Maybe he should forget about Michelle and the problems they were having and focus on what needed doing. Hugh had asked him if he could work a report about the abandoned baby into the coming week's programme. There had been a lot of interest surrounding the case and the public were keen to know more.

He had cleared it with the police and the hospital authorities, and was planning on including a short film, showing the baby in the nursery. He may as well make the arrangements while he had the chance.

Anna-Mae Lee, who was in charge of the nursery unit, let him in when he pressed the buzzer. He had been down to see the baby a couple of times and she smiled at him. 'Back again so soon, Dominic? You're becoming a regular visitor.'

'It must be because I enjoy the peace and quiet in here,' he replied with a grin.

Anna-Mae rolled her eyes. 'That's the one thing we're definitely short of in this department and especially today. I don't know what's got into all the babies this morning.'

Dominic laughed as he followed her to the glass-fronted nursery. There were at least twenty babies in there that day and they all seemed to be crying. The noise was tremendous. 'Do you get some days that are worse than others, then?'

'Yes. Nobody knows why it happens. Some days it's not too bad and other days the whole lot scream from morning till night and you can't seem to pacify them.'

Anna-Mae grinned as she keyed in the security code and opened the nursery door. 'I hope you've got strong nerves!'

Dominic groaned as the noise level increased by several decibels as he entered the room. 'I think I need strong ears not strong nerves. What a din! How's our little fellow doing, anyway?'

'Fine. In fact, he's the only one who hasn't given us any trouble today.' Anna-Mae led the way to the baby's crib and laughed. 'Look, fast asleep. What a little poppet. If only the others would follow his example.'

Dominic smiled as he looked down at the tiny child. The baby was lying on his back, his hands flung out above his head, his black lashes made tiny fans on his downy cheeks. He was dressed in a pale blue sleepsuit with a tiny white bonnet covering his head to help retain his body heat. He looked so contented that Dominic found himself mentally crossing his fingers that his life would continue that way after the rotten start he'd had. If any child needed a bit of luck on his side then this one did.

'He's coming along beautifully,' he told Anna-Mae. 'Have you heard about his mum? How is she?'

'She's still very weak. We took him down to see her this morning but she didn't show any interest in him, I'm afraid.'

Anna-Mae sighed as she ran a gentle finger down the baby's cheek. 'She wouldn't even look at him. She just rolled over and closed her eyes when we pushed his crib nearer to her bed.'

'Poor kid. This must be a lot for her to cope with,' Dominic said sadly. 'Have the staff in the surgical ward found out her name yet?'

'No, she won't tell them anything, won't even speak most of the time, apparently. The police are checking the missing persons' register in the hope that she might have been reported missing somewhere in the country, but if they can't make any headway they'll have to publish her photo in the papers.'

'I expect they're trying to avoid that if possible,' he said flatly. 'The last thing she needs at the moment is a whole load of reporters hassling her, not to mention the repercussions it could cause. Having a baby outside marriage tends to be frowned on in Asian circles and her family will most probably be horrified when they find out.'

'You think that's why she abandoned the baby?' Anna-Mae said thoughtfully.

'I think it's had a lot to do with it. Imagine being her

age and having to cope with the fact that you're pregnant when you know that it goes against everything your family believes in.' He shook his head sadly. 'That's why it's so important to provide sex education for teenagers from all cultures.'

'I saw your programme last year when you covered the subject,' Anna-Mae told him. 'It was great. I've got teenage twins and they both watched it and said how informative it was.'

'Good. That's what we were aiming for. Anyway, what I came for was to see if you would mind if I did a short piece about the baby,' he explained. 'There's been a lot of interest from the public so we thought we would give people an update on his progress.'

'There's no problem as far as I can see. Just give me a call when you want to do the filming. Are you going to mention anything about his mother?'

'No. I certainly don't want to make the situation more difficult for her. If there's a chance that she can be reconciled with her family quietly and without any fuss then that's what we need to work towards. Then it will be up to them what they do about this little fellow.'

'Well, I can't see there'll be a shortage of people wanting to adopt him if it comes to that,' Anna-Mae said, leading the way from the nursery. 'The switchboard has been jammed with calls from people offering him a home.'

'It's good to know that he'll have a secure future no matter what happens with his mum,' Dominic said thankfully.

He thanked Anna-Mae and went back to the A and E unit. He felt a lot better for the breathing space and for having to focus on someone else's problems rather than his own injured feelings. His concerns about Michelle seemed very insignificant in comparison. It made him realise that there had to be a solution if he tried hard enough to find it.

There was a spring in his step as he crossed the department. Ruth obviously noticed his upbeat mood because she grinned as he passed. 'Do I take it that you and Michelle have ironed out your differences, then?'

'Sorry?' Dominic frowned.

'I suggested to Michelle that she should talk about her concerns over the filming with you. I mean, it's obvious that she's got a bit of a bee in her bonnet about you being here, and I thought it would make sense if she told you what was worrying her.'

Ruth looked at him uncertainly. 'She did mention it, didn't she? I just assumed that she must have done because you're looking so much more cheerful. We've all noticed that there seems to be a bit of an atmosphere when you two are together, and I expect it's a relief to be able to get everything sorted out.'

'Ahem...yes.' Maybe it was wrong not to come clean and admit that Michelle hadn't made any mention of her concerns, but it was too tempting to miss out on the opportunity to find out what was really wrong with her. 'Michelle is worried about appearing on television?'

'That's right.' Ruth sighed. 'I told her that she was crazy and that she'll come across exactly as what she is—a wonderfully dedicated and caring doctor—but she seemed very edgy about the idea. Still, I suppose that's the type of person she is. She's not one who wants to be in the limelight all the time. It's hard to believe that we've worked together for the past five years because I know absolutely zilch about her. Maybe this will help to bring her out of her shell.'

'Maybe,' he echoed as Ruth hurried away to deal with

a screaming toddler who had just thrown up all over
Reception.

Was that the explanation for the way Michelle had
been behaving? he wondered as he took a card out of
the file and went to summon his next patient. Did it stem
from her fear of publicity?

It made sense in one way but didn't in another.
Dominic sighed as he realised that once again he was
trying to answer questions without any real knowledge
to work from. He simply didn't know Michelle well
enough, but he would. By the time he left St Justin's in
a few weeks' time he would know exactly what made
the mysterious Michelle Roberts tick!

'That's a good boy, Joseph. Just keep really still....
There!'

Michelle smiled as she held up a bright green bead
on the end of the forceps. Three-year-old Joseph
Delrenico had decided that his nose was the perfect place
to hide the bead. His anxious mother had tried everything she could think of to dislodge it before she'd admitted defeat and brought the little boy to hospital.

'Oh, no, you don't, young man!' Michelle quickly
moved the bead out of the child's reach as he made a
grab for it. She dropped it in the bin then turned to the
child's mother.

'Joseph should be fine now, but if you've got any
more of those beads lying around the house I'd put them
somewhere safe where he can't get at them.'

'They're going straight in the bin,' Angelina
Delrenico told her, taking a firm hold of the wriggling
toddler as he tried to get off her lap. 'I didn't even remember putting them in the drawer until I found him
sitting on the floor, playing with them.'

'You're quite sure he couldn't have swallowed any?' Michelle checked.

'No, he hasn't. I made sure of that before I brought him here. There was just one bead missing, the one he had pushed up his nose. Why on earth would he want to do that?'

'Now, that's a question I can't answer,' Michelle replied with a laugh as she walked the young mother out of the cubicle. 'Small children seem to have a passion for putting things where they aren't supposed to go. I've retrieved more beads, coins, hair-pins and buttons from various places than I can count since I've been working here!'

She made her way to the desk after Angelina had thanked her and left. There was still a queue of people waiting to be seen but she was glad that the afternoon had been so busy. At least while she'd been working she'd had little chance to think about what had happened that lunchtime.

She sighed as she picked up the next folder from the basket on the end of the desk. She had a horrible feeling that she might have made a fool of herself by rushing off like that, but there was little she could do about it. At least it seemed to have achieved one objective because Dominic had kept well clear of her all afternoon long.

As though thinking about him had somehow conjured him up, he suddenly appeared. Michelle felt a ripple run down her spine when he reached around her to take a folder and his arm brushed her shoulder. She tried not to react but she could tell from the look he shot her before he made his way back to the cubicles that he had felt her flinch.

She sighed because she knew that he must be won-

dering what was wrong with her. Nobody jumped like
that all the time unless there was a reason for them doing
so. The thought that she was inciting his curiosity by
behaving that way was more than she could bear, but
she seemed powerless to do anything about it.

She called in her next patient, a young man called
Gareth Jones who had managed to push a garden fork
through his foot while he'd been digging on his allot-
ment. His foot was badly swollen and it took Michelle
and Sandra Hunt, their nurse practitioner, some time to
get his boot off. Though clearly in pain, Gareth seemed
upset that his boot would be further ruined because it
needed to be cut off his foot.

Michelle smiled commiseratingly at him as Sandra set
to work with a workmanlike pair of shears kept specifically for such a contingency. 'I know what a nuisance
it must be, but we need to take a look at your foot, Mr
Jones. You can always get another pair of boots but you
can't grow another foot.'

'I know. It's just that I only bought them last month
and they weren't cheap.' He grimaced as Sandra finished
slicing through the leather. 'I don't think they'll be much
good after this.'

'Not unless you happen to know a good cobbler who
can stitch them back together again.'

Michelle gently peeled off the man's blood-soaked
sock and frowned when she saw the puncture mark in
the top of his foot. It looked as though the tine of the
fork had gone straight through the flesh and tendons then
stopped when it had hit the cuboid bone.

She carefully raised his foot and checked the sole but
there was no exit wound. 'I'm going to have to send you
for an X-ray. We need to see if the bone has been dam-
aged.'

'Is it a problem if it has been broken?' he asked worriedly. He looked at the bloody wound on his foot and gulped. 'I'm sorry, Doc, but I feel a bit funny. It's seeing all that blood...'

Michelle leapt forward as he suddenly keeled over. She managed to get her shoulder under him and support him until Sandra was able to help her get him safely back onto the bed. She sighed as the nurse quickly raised the metal sides on the bed.

'That took me by surprise. One minute he was fine, the next he'd gone.'

Sandra chuckled. 'I thought he was going to squash you. You must be stronger than you look. He's no lightweight.'

'Don't I know it?' She grimaced as she flexed her shoulder. 'Anyway, there's not a lot we can do until he's had an X-ray. If the bone is broken he might need a cast, and there's bound to be some tendon damage which might need to be repaired surgically. Send him through to X-Ray when he comes round and we can go from there.'

'Right. I'll get this cleaned up a bit while he's napping, then I'd better check if his tetanus jabs are up to date.' Sandra grinned wickedly. 'I wonder how he is with needles.'

'Hopefully better than he is with the sight of blood,' Michelle replied ruefully. She stepped out of the cubicle then gasped when she cannoned into someone who was passing.

'Sorry,' she began, turning to apologise for her clumsiness. Her eyes suddenly found themselves staring into a pair of all too familiar green ones and she felt her stomach lurch sickeningly. When Dominic reached out and put his hands gently on her shoulders she couldn't move a muscle. She seemed to be frozen into place, held there by the intensity of his gaze, by the feel of his hands resting on her. All around them the hustle and bustle carried on, but it felt as though they were removed from it all as they stood there looking at one another.

'Are you all right?' he asked softly.

'Yes.' She took a deep breath and stepped back so that he was forced to release her, but she knew that he was as shaken as she was by what had happened. It was almost a relief when Ruth came hurrying along the corridor to tell them that there was an emergency admission on the way in.

'I'll take it.'

Dominic stepped forward, neatly forestalling her offer to go. Michelle watched him hurrying towards the front entrance then closed her eyes. She wasn't sure what had happened just then, or even if anything had. But all of a sudden she knew that she couldn't keep on like this. She couldn't avoid Dominic yet she couldn't bear to be around him and run the risk of breaking her vow. It was a cleft stick and she was firmly placed right in the middle with no way to turn.

'You all right, Michelle?'

She blinked when she heard Sandra speaking to her. 'Fine. I was just taking a breather.'

Fortunately the other woman seemed to accept what she said without question as she went to summon a porter to take Gareth Jones to the X-ray department. Michelle squared her shoulders then made her way to the front desk. She was due for a break but she preferred to keep on working rather than spend the time sitting on her own in the staffroom, thinking about what had happened.

She reached for a folder from the basket but stopped

when she felt someone touch her shoulder. She swung round, feeling panic setting in when she realised it was Dominic so that it was a moment before she understood what he was telling her.

'Carmen is here?' she repeated blankly. 'But why? What's happened?'

'The ambulance brought her in just now.'

She saw him take a deep breath and her heart seemed to stop when she saw the compassion in his eyes. 'She's had a stroke, Michelle, and it isn't looking good, I'm afraid.'

'Time of death four forty-five.'

Dominic glanced around the resuscitation room. Carmen Rivera had died without regaining consciousness, and he could tell that everyone involved felt as sad as he did. 'Thanks, everyone. That was a real team effort.'

'Do you want me to tell Michelle?' Ruth asked quietly, drawing the sheet over the old lady's body.

'No, I'll do it. It's going to hit her hard because she was very fond of Carmen.'

'Did I hear you mention something about the old lady being Michelle's neighbour?' Ruth asked curiously, as she followed him from the room.

'That's right.'

Dominic sighed as he looked towards the office. He had insisted that Michelle should wait in there until he fetched her. He'd had the devil of a job convincing her that it would be better if she left it to him to take care of the old lady, but she had been in no fit state to deal with the case after the shock she'd had. He could imagine how upset she was going to be on hearing that

Carmen had died, but he wouldn't dream of allowing anyone else to break the news to her.

'I met her the other night when I took Michelle home. She seemed a really feisty old lady.'

'You took Michelle home?' Ruth looked at him in amazement. 'That must be a first.'

'What do you mean?' he asked, frowning when he saw the surprise on the woman's face.

'Michelle never invites anyone to her home. In all the time we've worked together she hasn't once asked me to pop round for a coffee or a glass of wine after we've finished our shift.' Ruth shook her head in amazement. 'So how come you got an invite, Dominic, and nobody else has?'

'I'm not sure,' he said lightly, although he had to admit that he was shocked by the revelation. He had suspected that Michelle didn't mix with her colleagues, but never to have invited anyone to her flat struck him as very odd behaviour. 'I suppose I should consider myself highly honoured?'

'Too right you should!' Ruth replied, before she hurried away as Amy summoned her.

Dominic made his way to the office. He wasn't looking forward to what he had to do but it would be best to get it over with as soon as possible. Michelle was standing by the window and she turned when she heard the door opening.

He felt a wave of tenderness wash over him when he saw the fear in her beautiful grey eyes. Closing the door, he went over to her and took her hands, holding them tightly in the probably vain hope that it would comfort her to know that he was there if she needed him.

'I'm very sorry, Michelle. Carmen died a few minutes

ago. We did everything we could but it just wasn't to be.'

She closed her eyes and he saw her throat move convulsively. 'Di-did she regain consciousness?'

'No.' He squeezed her hands when he felt the tremor that ran through her. 'She wouldn't have known what was happening, if that's any comfort. It would have been like a light being switched off.'

'Thank you.' She tried to smile but he could see tears welling from her eyes. 'It makes it a bit easier to know that she wasn't in pain or afraid.'

Her voice broke on a sob and Dominic sighed as he pulled her into his arms. 'She wasn't.'

He held her against him, feeling her slender body shaking as the sobs racked her. She felt so small and defenceless that he was overwhelmed by a need to protect her.

He smoothed his hand over her hair, feeling its silkiness against his palm, smelling the faint scent of apples from the shampoo she had used. Usually he had no difficulty finding the right words to say in any given situation, but for some reason he felt at a loss to know what to say to comfort Michelle. It seemed easier to fall back on actions rather than rely on words.

He drew her closer, nestling her small body against his as though he was offering her shelter and protection from all the cruelties she might encounter. He felt a sudden warmth flood him when he felt her arms go around his waist as she clung to him. In that moment he knew that he would do anything it took to make her trust him. He cared what happened to her. He cared probably more than he should and definitely more than was sensible, but that didn't alter how he felt.

She took a shuddering breath then let her arms fall to

her sides and stepped back. Dominic didn't try to hold
onto her because he knew that it would be the wrong
thing to do. That she had unbent enough to let him hold
her had been a miracle, and it would be pushing his luck
to ask for another one so soon. If he intended to make
any headway then he had to take things slowly, one step
at a time.

'I'd like to see her.'

'Of course. She's still in Resus so why don't you go
in and sit with her for a while?' he suggested, opening
the office door. 'It's quiet at the moment and nobody
will disturb you.'

'I'd like that,' she said softly. She crossed the corridor
and he saw her hesitate outside the resuscitation room
before she glanced back and smiled at him. 'Thank you,
Dominic. For everything you've done.'

'You're welcome, Michelle,' he said softly.

She didn't say anything else as she slipped into the
room and closed the door. She didn't need to. That smile
had been more than enough.

Dominic made his way to Reception in a daze. Bryan
Patterson said something to him and he answered. It
must have made sense because the registrar didn't look
alarmed, but for the life of him Dominic had no idea
what he had said. His mind seemed to be stuck at that
moment when Michelle had smiled at him. He realised
that he would have walked over hot coals or faced any
kind of peril if it meant she would look at him like that
again!

His heart gave a sudden lurch of terror. He'd had his
share of relationships over the years, but love was something that had eluded him so far. He hadn't deliberately
tried to avoid it because he was as open to the idea of
falling in love as he was to most things. He had simply

taken a relaxed view that it would happen when it happened and hadn't worried about it.

Now he could see that had been a big mistake. If he had laid down some guidelines, he wouldn't be faced with this dilemma.

Dominic swore softly under his breath. Of all the women in all the world, he had to be attracted to the one woman who didn't even like him.

Oh, hell!

CHAPTER SIX

MICHELLE dried her eyes then gently drew up the sheet. Carmen looked so serene lying there that she knew Dominic had told her the truth. The old lady had died peacefully and it was a comfort to know that.

She sighed as she left the room and recalled how kind he had been to her. Of course, he must be used to dealing with this kind of situation, but his sympathy and concern had seemed to go beyond what she might have expected. When he had held her in his arms she had been overwhelmed by a feeling of security. It was as though he had been trying to shelter her from the pain of her friend's loss and it had touched her deeply. Now, however, she had to rid her mind of thoughts like that because they were too seductive. Wishing that Dominic could shelter her from all life's problems wasn't an option.

'Hey, are you OK?' Ruth came over and impulsively gave her a hug. 'I'm so sorry about your friend, Michelle. Really I am. If there's anything I can do, you only have to say.'

'Thanks.' Michelle felt her eyes fill with tears again and hurriedly blinked them away. 'I really appreciate that, Ruth, but I'm fine.'

'Are you?' Ruth didn't look convinced. 'Why don't you tell Max that you're going home? It must have been a shock for you and I'm sure he'll understand.'

'No, it's fine, really.' She smiled bravely, touched by

the other woman's concern. 'I'd rather stay here and work. It will be better than sitting at home, brooding.'

'Well, you know best, of course. Sandra has arranged to have Carmen taken to the chapel. Is there anyone we need to get in touch with?' Ruth asked briskly, obviously deciding it was best to concentrate on practicalities.

'I'm not sure. She didn't have any family from what I could gather.' She frowned thoughtfully. 'I suppose I should phone the vicar of our local church. Carmen was a regular churchgoer and a keen member of the social club.'

'I'll do it,' Ruth said swiftly. She patted Michelle's hand. 'Just take it easy. You've had a shock and there's no point trying to pretend that it hasn't affected you.'

Michelle sighed as Ruth hurried away to make the phone call. It was kind of her to be so concerned but the last thing she wanted was to stand around, doing nothing.

She made for the reception desk, smiling when Amy and Bryan came over to say how sorry they were about what had happened. Even Mike Soames, the cameraman, gave her a hug. It was a bit overwhelming to be on the receiving end of so much concern because she wasn't used to it. It made her wonder all of a sudden if she had been wrong to keep everyone at a distance.

Stephen wouldn't have wanted her to isolate herself the way she had. His main concern had always been her happiness, yet she had felt a deep need to ensure that his memory would never be diminished. Now the thought that she might have made a mistake was so disturbing that she couldn't face it. She pushed it out of her mind as she went to summon her next patient.

Ten minutes later, Michelle was starting to wish that she had taken Ruth's advice and gone home. Although the majority of the people they dealt with were appreciative of their efforts, a few were downright rude. Donna Parsons was one of the latter, unfortunately.

Donna had punched her fist through a shop window, causing extensive damage to her hand and wrist. There were fragments of glass embedded in the flesh and Michelle also suspected that there might be some nerve and tendon damage. The patient had been brought into hospital by the police, who had been summoned by the shopkeeper after Donna had threatened him, and she was obviously intent on making as much trouble as possible for everyone concerned.

'Mind what you're doing, you silly cow!' she spat when Michelle gently turned over her hand to examine her palm. She smelt strongly of alcohol and Michelle sighed as she realised that would be a big problem if they needed to send her to Theatre.

'Just try to keep still,' she said quietly, positioning the magnifying glass directly over the woman's palm. 'I need to remove these splinters of glass. The local anaesthetic I gave you should have taken effect by now so it shouldn't be too painful.'

She gently tweezed out a sliver of glass then jumped when Donna screamed.

'That hurt! I thought you said I wouldn't feel anything.'

Michelle put down the tweezers and looked at her. 'It wouldn't hurt so much if you kept still.'

'How would you know?' Donna shot back, glaring at her. 'It isn't your hand that's being treated like a lump of meat. You doctors are all the same...'

'Everything all right in here?'

Michelle looked round when Dominic popped his head round the curtain. 'The patient is a little agitated,' she explained in a massive understatement that immediately brought a smile to his lips.

'You do surprise me.' He treated her to a look that made her heart start to race because there was such a feeling of intimacy about it. It was almost a relief when Donna gave an ear-splitting squeal.

'You're that doctor off the telly! Will *you* take a look at my hand? This silly cow doesn't have the faintest idea what she's doing!'

Michelle bit her lip to hold back the angry retort as Donna thrust out her hand for Dominic's inspection. He glanced at her and she could see the amusement in his eyes.

'Mind if I take a look?'

'Be my guest.'

She stripped off her gloves and tossed them into the waste sack before making a swift exit from the cubicle. The policeman waiting outside gave her a sympathetic smile, but it didn't make her feel any better. She wasn't sure why she was so annoyed. It really wasn't Dominic's fault that the patient had asked him to take over. However, she couldn't help feeling put out at having had her authority usurped that way.

She told Ruth that she was taking her break and went to the staffroom. It was almost time for the day shift to go off duty, but she still had another couple of hours to work. For the first time in her life, she found herself wishing that she could walk out and leave it all behind, but what would she have left if she did that? All she had was her work. Without it her life would be empty and meaningless.

It was a depressing thought and she blamed Dominic for making her think it. She had been perfectly happy until he had come along and upset everything. Damn him for causing all these problems, for creating this havoc!

'Is it safe to come in?'

She looked up when she heard his voice, feeling her heart lurch once again when she saw the wary expression on his face. There wasn't a doubt in her mind that he knew she was upset and that she was upset because of him, and she bitterly resented the fact that it made her feel so vulnerable. She didn't want to give this man that much power over her!

'You don't need to ask my permission,' she snapped, rising to her feet. 'It's up to you what you do.'

'Not if it's going to cause you a problem.'

'You aren't causing me any problems, I assure you.' She stalked to the door then froze when she heard him laugh. She glanced back and was shocked when she saw the sceptical look he gave her.

'So you keep saying, Michelle, but why do I have such difficulty believing you? Could it be that every time we try to talk it ends up with you running away?'

He took a deep breath yet his voice seemed to grate when he continued, making her shiver when she felt the vibrations from it rubbing along her nerves.

'Why are you so afraid to let yourself like me?'

Dominic hadn't known he was going to ask her that until the words had actually emerged from his lips. He felt every nerve in his body grow tense as he waited to hear what Michelle would say, even though he knew that the likelihood of her answering him truthfully was very slim.

'Because it would be a mistake.'

He wasn't sure who was the most surprised. He guessed from the shock on her face that she hadn't meant to come out with something so revealing. He took a quick step towards her then stopped when Max Hastings suddenly appeared.

'So here you are. Excellent! Saves me having to track you both down.' Max rubbed his hands, exuding *bonhomie* as he came into the room. 'I've just had a chap on the phone who's interested in the trauma surgeon's post. Tons of experience both here and in the States.'

He beamed at Dominic. 'It appears he watched your programme the other night and remembered seeing the advert for the job. Anyway, he was so impressed by our new facilities that he decided to phone me as soon as he had the chance. He's coming to look round the department tomorrow.'

'That's excellent,' Dominic said, trying to summon up a suitable degree of enthusiasm. 'You must be pleased.'

'Oh, I am. We've had a couple of people interested but none of them had had enough experience, unfortunately.' Max turned to Michelle. 'This chap sounds really promising.'

'That's good.' She gave them a quick smile, carefully avoiding looking at Dominic. 'I'd better get back to the fray.'

'And I'd better get a move on. I've a fundraising dinner tonight and I don't want to be late,' Max informed them, checking his watch.

Dominic took a deep breath as they both left the room. He couldn't believe how frustrated he felt. He'd been on the verge of making some headway, only to have it whipped out of his reach.

He went out into the corridor but there was no sign of Michelle anywhere about. The curtains were drawn on several of the cubicles and the treatment-room door was closed as well. Frankly, he balked at the idea of tracking her down because he knew that she wouldn't appreciate it. He would just have to curb his impatience and hope that he would make another breakthrough soon.

His stoicism lasted no longer than the time it took him to drive home. He had bought the house in Richmond the previous year and usually loved going home at the end of a busy day. Even when he had work to do—as he had that night—it was good to go in and shut his own front door on the world and its problems.

The trouble was that this problem couldn't be shut out. He kept hearing Michelle's voice over and over again, telling him that it would be a mistake to let herself like him. Why? What had she meant?

He turned the car around. He wouldn't have a minute's peace until he found out the answer, although he wasn't foolish enough to think that it would be easy to get the truth out of her. She'd had time to shore up her defences and it would take a lot of persuasion to make her open up again, but it would be worth it if he finally found out the truth.

It was raining hard when Michelle left the hospital at a little after ten. She pulled up her collar and hurried down the drive. She was anxious to get home. Dulcie would be going frantic because no one had been in to give her any supper.

She sighed sadly as she thought about Carmen. She was going to miss the old lady a great deal and not just because of all the favours Carmen had done her over the years. It had been good to have someone to talk to, someone who was interested in what she did. Once again she found herself wondering if she had been silly to isolate herself the way she had done. Maybe she should start being a bit more friendly towards the people she worked with, accept their frequent offers to join them for a drink at the pub after work? It would make a nice change to go out rather than spend every night on her own in the flat.

'Michelle.'

She jumped when she heard Dominic calling her name. She glanced round uncertainly and felt her heart jerk to a stop when she saw him standing in the shadows beside the gates. There was a film of moisture glistening on his dark hair and the shoulders of his jacket were soaked. He had obviously been standing there for some time, waiting for her, but what did he want?

'I wanted a word with you, Michelle,' he said quietly as he came over to her. He searched her face and she felt a shiver run down her spine when she saw how grave he looked.

'If it's about work, surely it can wait until tomorrow,' she said shortly, brushing past him. 'It's been a long day, Dominic, and I'm tired…'

'I want to know what you meant earlier about it being a mistake to let yourself like me.'

She froze, wondering sickly how she could have made such a slip. Had he caught her off guard, perhaps? Or had it simply been too difficult to hold back the truth?

She heard him sigh when she didn't say anything. 'I know I shouldn't have come. I know I shouldn't be asking you to explain, but it's important to me, Michelle. I need to know what you meant!'

She turned to look at him and she could see at once that he was telling her the truth. Dominic really cared what she had meant by that statement. All of a sudden she knew that she wanted to explain everything to him—about Stephen and why it was so important that she do the right thing. And maybe by explaining it to him it

would help her get everything straight in her own mind.
Anything would be better than this confusion she had
felt of late.

'All right, then, but if you want to talk to me I'm
afraid we shall have to go to my flat. I need to give
Dulcie her supper.'

'Fine by me.' He gave her a quick smile and there
was such gentleness in his eyes that her stalled heart
suddenly started beating again. 'I'll even face the
dreaded feline if it means we can get this sorted out once
and for all, Michelle.'

'You might regret saying that,' she warned, trying to
make light of what was happening.

'The only thing I'll regret is letting this situation continue.' He took a deep breath and she sensed that he was
deliberately reining in his emotions to keep everything
low-key. 'I want us to be friends, Michelle. It's as simple
as that.'

It didn't feel simple to her but she didn't admit that.
She had made her decision and she wasn't going to go
back on it. Dominic led the way to his car and opened
the door for her to get in.

Michelle rested her head against the soft leather seat
as he started the engine, feeling her heart beating inside
her chest. It reminded her of the night she had sat in her
flat, listening to Dominic's footsteps running down the
stairs. She'd known then that this man was going to create problems in her life and she'd been right. But suddenly she didn't resent it. Maybe it was time to talk
about the past and look towards the future.

Dulcie set up a tremendous racket the minute she heard
the key in the lock. Michelle paused before opening the
door. 'I think you'd better let me go in first and give her

some supper. She might be a bit better tempered once she's been fed.'

'Only "might"?' One black brow quirked and he smiled ruefully at her. 'Why doesn't that fill me with confidence?'

She laughed softly, feeling some of her tension ease a little. 'She can be really sweet sometimes.'

'Hmm, I'll take your word for it.' He leant against the wall and folded his arms. 'Give me a shout when the coast's clear.'

Michelle chuckled softly as she hurried inside and made straight for the kitchen. Dulcie hissed her displeasure but she was soon mollified when Michelle opened a tin of her favourite sardines and scooped them into her bowl. Leaving the animal happily eating her supper, she went to let in Dominic.

'I've bribed her with a dish of her favourite sardines. She should be sweetness and light in a few minutes' time.'

'I won't hold my breath,' he said lightly, following her along the hall.

Michelle led the way into the living room and quickly turned on the lamps then slipped off her jacket. 'Would you like a drink? I've got a bottle of wine in the fridge.'

He shook his head. 'No, thanks. I'm driving so I won't have anything alcoholic, but don't let that stop you from having a glass if you want one. You probably need it after the day you've had.'

'No, it's fine.' She sat on the sofa then stood up again almost immediately. 'Let me hang up your jacket. It's soaked.'

'It will be fine over the chair.' He draped it over the back of a nearby chair then sat down and regarded her levelly. 'Don't be nervous, Michelle. I promise you there's no need. Anything you tell me won't go beyond these four walls if that's what you're afraid of.'

'It isn't!' she shot back, then sighed. 'Sorry. I don't mean to snap all the time. I'm just not used to talking about myself and it's difficult.'

'I realise that. Ruth told me earlier today that she knows very little about you despite the fact that you two have worked together for a number of years.'

He leant back in the chair, the light from a nearby lamp lending an unaccustomed gentleness to his features. Or maybe the gentleness had been there all along and she had failed to notice it before? Had she been too busy disliking him to see beyond the confident face he presented to the world?

It was a disquieting thought, especially right then. 'She was telling you the truth. I've made a point of not getting too friendly with the people I work with.'

'Why, Michelle? You must have had a reason for it. I've seen how you behave with the patients and it's obvious that you have a great deal of empathy with them.'

'It's easier to relate to them because nine times out of ten I'll never see them again.' She shrugged, wondering if he would understand.

'So they aren't a threat to you? Is that what you mean?' he prompted.

'Yes, I suppose so.' She rubbed her hands up and down her arms, feeling suddenly chilled despite the fact that it wasn't cold in the room. 'I just want to concentrate on doing my job. It's important to me to do it to the very best of my ability.'

'But that doesn't mean you should cut yourself off from everything else. You could still do your job and have a private life. You deserve to have some pleasure in your life, something other than work.'

'It wouldn't feel right. It would seem as though I was trying to forget about Stephen and all the sacrifices he made for me.' She shook her head. 'I couldn't live with myself if I let that happen!'

'Who's Stephen?'

She heard the shock in his voice but there was nothing she could do about it right then when the pain seemed so fresh and raw all over again. 'Stephen was my husband. He died ten years ago, a month after I graduated from med school.'

Dominic could feel the blood drumming in his ears so that for a moment he felt quite dizzy. Michelle was sitting hunched up in the chair with an expression of such pain on her face that it almost broke his heart to see it. However, he knew instinctively that the last thing she needed was his sympathy.

'How did he die? He couldn't have been very old, I don't imagine.'

He was rather pleased by the calmness of his tone because he felt far from calm if the truth be told. The news that Michelle had been married had come like a bolt from the blue. But it wasn't his feelings that were the issue but hers. His heart spasmed again when he heard her take a shaky breath that hinted at how difficult she was finding it to talk about what had happened, even after all this time.

'He was twenty-four, the same age as me. He had a brain tumour and by the time it was diagnosed it was too late to do anything about it.'

'It must have been dreadful for you,' he said softly, fighting the urge he felt to get up and go to her because he knew there was little he could offer her in the way of comfort. The thought was bitterly painful.

'I think I was in a daze for months afterwards, which

was probably a blessing. I couldn't really believe what had happened. I used to wake up in the night and reach for him...'

She broke off and swallowed. 'What made it particularly hard was that Stephen and I had grown up together. I not only lost the man I loved but my best friend as well.'

'I can't imagine what you went through,' he said truthfully.

'It was hard. At one point I thought that I would never get over losing him, but then I realised that it would be wrong to give up. Stephen had worked so hard to help me through college and if I gave up then it would have all been in vain.'

She ran her hands over her face and he could see the glisten of tears on her cheeks. 'Stephen and I were brought up in care, you see. My mother died when I was fifteen and there was no one to look after me so I was sent to a children's home. Stephen had been put into care when he was a baby and although he'd had a number of foster-homes over the years, nobody had wanted to adopt him.' She smiled faintly. 'He'd been a bit of a handful.'

'So you two struck up a friendship while you were in the home?' he prompted when she stopped.

'He took me under his wing and looked after me. There was a lot of bullying in the home, and I was very quiet so I became a target until Stephen stepped in.' She sighed. 'I came to rely on him totally so when he suggested that we should get married after we left the home, I agreed immediately. He knew how desperate I was to go to med school and train to be a doctor, so he offered to support me while I studied.'

'Surely you would have been eligible for a grant,' he pointed out.

'Oh, yes. But you try living off a grant and buying everything you need—the textbooks, the equipment, and so on. Stephen got a job with a haulage firm. He worked horrendously long hours but he never complained.' She smiled. 'He said he was happy to do it because then I could keep him in luxury when I qualified.'

'He sounds like a great bloke,' he observed softly, feeling an ache in his heart even as he said that.

'He was kind and gentle, and wonderfully supportive. I wouldn't have got through college if it hadn't been for him, encouraging me, telling me that I could do it.' She took a deep breath and looked him straight in the eye. 'And if it hadn't been for me wanting to be a doctor, he might be alive today.'

'What on earth do you mean by that?' Dominic couldn't hide his surprise and he saw her eyes well up with tears.

'If he hadn't been so busy trying to earn enough money to support us, he might have paid more attention to his own health. He'd started having headaches—really, really bad ones, I mean. I kept telling him to go and see the doctor but he always found some excuse, usually that he was working. I was studying for my finals at the time and I was so caught up in them that I didn't pay enough attention to what was happening.'

She ran the back of her hand over her face but more tears replaced the ones she had wiped away. 'By the time he went for a CT scan the tumour was too big for them to operate. He died two weeks later and it was all my fault, you see. Stephen died because he wanted me to have this chance to do the job I had always longed to do. That's why I can't let anything interfere with my work!'

'And that includes having a relationship with another man?' he said hollowly, already guessing what her answer would be.

'I could never betray Stephen's memory that way. It wouldn't be right.'

'Do you honestly believe that Stephen would want you to do this?' he said hotly. He felt sick about what he had heard. Obviously, it explained such a lot, like the way she had berated him for having left medicine. However, the thought that she was *punishing* herself for something that hadn't been her fault was more than he could bear.

'What do you mean?'

'You said what a kind and considerate person Stephen was, so do you really think that he would be happy to know that you were living like this, cut off from other people?'

'That has nothing to do with it,' she began, but he didn't give her the chance to finish because it was too important that he make her understand the mistake she was making.

'It has everything to do with it, Michelle. Stephen wouldn't want you to go through life being lonely.' His voice gentled when he saw the distress on her face. 'Would he?'

'I...I don't suppose so,' she whispered.

'Then you must do something about it.' He stood up and went to crouch in front of her chair, willing her to believe him because it seemed so important that he convince her. He covered her cold hands with his and held them tightly.

'You need friends, Michelle, people you can turn to

when life gets tough, people whose company you can enjoy. It won't get in the way of you doing your job properly. It will just make your life better.'

He took a deep breath, wondering if he was completely crazy to say this when he knew in his heart that it wasn't what he wanted. He wanted more than this, a lot more, but after what he'd heard it seemed even less likely that it would happen.

'Will you let me be your friend, Michelle?'

CHAPTER SEVEN

'Is THAT what you really want, Dominic? To be my friend?'

Michelle felt as though she could drown in the concern she saw in his eyes. It warmed her to know that anyone cared this much about her, but she was a little afraid to take it at face value.

'Yes. And I know that the rest of the folk at St Justin's feel exactly the same.' He gave her hands a final squeeze and stood up.

She bit back a sigh, wondering why she felt disappointed. Was it the fact that he had equated himself with her colleagues at the hospital when she wanted his friendship to mean something special?

She shrugged aside that thought as she saw him take his jacket off the chair. 'Do you have to go so soon?'

'I don't want to outstay my welcome, Michelle. I know how difficult this must have been for you and I think you need some space.'

'Maybe you're right,' she conceded, getting up to see him out. She gave a gasp of dismay when Dulcie suddenly appeared. 'Oh, careful!'

Dominic smiled grimly as he bent and offered the cat his clenched fist to sniff. 'She's going to have to get used to me at some point. I refuse to keep on skulking outside on the landing every time I visit you.'

'So you intend to come back?' she queried softly.

'If you'll let me.'

'Of course.' She rushed on before her courage deserted her, although surprisingly it was easier to say the words than she'd feared it would be. 'You're welcome to visit me any time you want to, Dominic.'

'Good.' He gave her a quick smile then laughed when the cat rolled onto her back in a blatant attempt to make him stroke her. 'Do you think this is a sign that she's accepted me or a trick to catch me off guard?'

'Knowing Dulcie, it could be either,' she replied lightly.

She followed him into the hall and opened the front door. 'Thank you for coming tonight. I appreciate it.'

'So long as it's helped to iron out a few problems, that's the main thing, Michelle.'

'It has. And I'm sorry if I've been...well, so prickly with you. I promise that I'll try harder in the future.' She groaned when she realised how that sounded. 'I wasn't trying to imply it would be an effort in case you were wondering.'

'I wasn't. What's that saying about friends not having to say they are sorry all the time?' He bent and kissed her lightly on the forehead. 'Say what you want because I don't want you to change. I like you just the way you are, prickles and all!'

She couldn't help laughing at that. 'I don't think so! Anyway, I'll see you tomorrow, I expect.'

'I won't be in until the afternoon,' he warned her. 'I need to run through the film we'll be using on the next edition of *Health Matters*.' He rolled his eyes. 'If I let Hugh have his way it will be non-stop gore from start to finish. Whilst that might go down well with the younger members of our audience, I would prefer to present a more balanced view of the work you do.'

'Are you thinking of including a clip on Donna Parsons, the woman who put her fist through that plate-glass window?' She smiled sweetly but her eyes were glinting with mischief. 'She seemed really impressed by you.'

'Don't remind me!' he groaned. 'I nearly had to fight her off. Thank heavens that policeman was waiting outside, that's all I can say. And, yes, I shall be including a clip of her because it's important to remind the public what A and E staff have to put up with. It isn't all smiley-happy people gushing with thanks.'

'I wish!' she declared ruefully. She waited until he had reached the stairs then closed the door and went back inside. Going to the window, she watched him walking to his car. He paused and looked up, waving when he saw her at the window.

Michelle waved back then moved away from the window as he drove away. She let out a sigh of relief. She felt so much better knowing that she could be friends with Dominic rather than enemies.

She frowned. She'd never really seen him as an enemy, though, not even in the beginning. She'd been worried about the effect he would have on the department, then concerned about the effect he seemed to have had on her. It had been as difficult to put him into any single category then as it was now to say that he was simply a friend.

Calling Dominic a friend didn't seem to be quite enough.

'RTA arriving in five minutes. Three casualties reported, one of them a pregnant woman. Looks like it's action stations!'

Michelle shook her head when she heard the excitement in John Peterson's voice as he came back from answering the emergency phone. 'You will soon learn to appreciate the quiet times,' she warned him. 'Give it a few more weeks and you'll be as relieved as the rest of us are when nothing much happens.'

'Probably,' he conceded. 'But you have to admit that it's been *boring* this morning. I've never seen the place so empty.'

'I think word must have got round that Dominic isn't here,' Ruth suggested with a twinkle in her eyes. 'Everyone has decided to wait until this afternoon when he gets back before they do themselves any real damage!'

Everyone laughed as they left the staffroom and went their various ways. Michelle headed straight for Resus, leaving it to the others to meet the ambulances when they arrived. She wanted to be certain that everything was prepared in readiness for the incoming patients.

She smiled as she thought about what Ruth had said while she set up the foetal monitor beside one of the beds. It did seem strange that they had seen so few patients that morning but, occasionally, it just happened that they had a slack period. She didn't believe that it had anything to do with Dominic's absence any more than Ruth did, but she had to admit that she'd missed having him around that morning. Was it because she felt so much better now that they'd got things straight after their talk last night?

She had no time to dwell on the question because the first patient arrived just then. She ran to the door as Si Watson and Lisa Prentice pushed the trolley into the room.

'Sheryl Morris, age twenty-two. Front-seat passenger in one of the cars,' Lisa rattled out breathlessly as they lined up the trolley beside the bed. 'She's thirty-five weeks pregnant and it's her first baby. Fractured left tibia and fibula. No sign of any other injuries.'

'Right. Let's get her onto the bed.' Michelle bent over the pretty brunette. 'I'm Michelle Roberts, one of the doctors. We're going to move you onto the bed now, Sheryl.'

'My baby,' the girl gasped. 'Is it all right? I can't feel it moving!' Her hand fluttered over her abdomen. 'I've got this terrible pain...'

'I'm going to check you out as soon as we have you on the bed,' Michelle told her soothingly, then glanced round. 'On my count—one, two, three.'

They quickly transferred Sheryl to the bed and Michelle glanced at Amy, who was assisting her. 'Let's remove her lower garments and attach the foetal monitor.'

They worked together to save time because it was imperative that they find out if the baby was in distress. The other casualties—two young men—had arrived by then, but she left it to Bryan and Max to deal with them.

Michelle attached the foetal ultrasound transmitter to Sheryl's abdomen and turned on the monitor, frowning in concern when she couldn't detect a heartbeat at first. She adjusted its position and sighed in relief when there was a familiar beeping noise.

'The baby's fine, Sheryl,' she said, squeezing her hand. 'If I'm not mistaken, though, you're in labour and that's why he isn't moving about as much as he was.'

'But I'm not due for another five weeks,' the girl cried.

Michelle bent and examined her. 'You're almost fully dilated. It's probably been the shock of the accident that has triggered labour, but don't worry—everything will be fine.'

She turned to Amy, who was looking a little stunned at the thought of a baby being born in the casualty unit.

'Can you phone Maternity and tell them what's happened? We're going to need an incubator down here. And ask them if they can send someone to help, please.'

Amy hurried away while Michelle quickly checked Sheryl over, mentally crossing her fingers that there wouldn't be anything seriously wrong with her. Obviously her fractured tibia and fibula would need attending to, but the temporary support the paramedics had fitted should suffice for now. Their main concern had to be the baby and its imminent arrival.

Sheryl suddenly gasped. 'Oh, I think that was a contraction!'

'Did you attend any antenatal classes?' Michelle asked gently.

'Yes, but Lee was always with me. He's supposed to help me breathe and I don't think I can manage without him!' She was obviously getting upset and that was the last thing Michelle wanted to happen because of the effect it might have on the child. She squeezed Sheryl's hand again.

'Try to stay calm. I'll see if I can get a message to Lee and ask him to come to the hospital. How do I get in touch with him?'

'He was driving the car,' Sheryl explained, closing her eyes and groaning as another pain racked her.

Michelle's heart sank because she had no idea what kind of a state the girl's partner was in. She looked up when Amy came back to tell her that someone would be down soon from the maternity unit. 'That's great. Just stay here with Sheryl for a moment.'

She hurried over to the nearest bed and drew Max to one side. 'What's the patient's name?' she said urgently.

'Lee Gerard—why?' Max asked with a frown.

'Because his girlfriend is about to give birth and she's

panicking because she wants him with her. How bad
is he?'

'Well, he's conscious, if that's what you're asking.
He's got a couple of broken ribs, a fractured clavicle and
whiplash injuries to the neck. That's what I've found so
far but there could be something else.'

'Do you think he's well enough to help? The baby's
pre-term and the last thing I want is the mother getting
upset,' she explained.

'I suppose you'd better ask him,' Max said with a hint
of resignation.

Michelle hurried to the bed and bent down to speak
to the young man. 'Sheryl is having the baby, Lee, and
she wants you with her. Do you feel up to it? We can
move your bed next to hers and you can talk her through
her breathing.'

'But it's not due for weeks yet!' he declared in dismay.

'I know that, but the shock of the accident must have
sent Sheryl into labour. It's too late to give her much in
the way of pain relief so her breathing is going to be
really important.' She glanced round when she heard the
girl scream as another contraction began.

'Of course I'll help,' Lee said swiftly. 'Anything, so
long as Sheryl and the baby are all right.'

'Thanks.'

Michelle rewarded him with a smile then quickly explained to the others what was happening. It took very
little time to move Lee's bed and position it close
enough so that he could hold Sheryl's hand. She sighed
in relief when she heard him leading Sheryl through the
routine they had learned together at antenatal classes.
That was one hurdle over. Now all they needed was for

the baby to make its appearance, which it did in record time.

It was a little girl, very small but absolutely perfect. Everyone held their breath as Michelle laid her on the bed and quickly cleared the mucus from her mouth. She gently flicked the soles of the child's feet with the tip of her finger, smiling as a ripple of applause ran around the room when the little girl gave a shrill wail. She looked round when the door opened and Amanda Bennet, the obstetric registrar, arrived.

'You're a few seconds too late.'

'So I see,' Amanda said drily. She glanced at the young couple, holding hands between their respective beds, and shook her head. 'This place gets more like a madhouse every day.'

Michelle laughed. 'You mean you wouldn't want to trade places with me and work here?'

'No way!' Amanda declared, quickly clamping and cutting the baby's cord. 'I know my limitations, thank you very much. I shall stick to my mums and babies, and leave the rest to you brave souls.'

She whisked the infant into the portable incubator she had brought with her, then had a word with the parents to tell them that the infant was being taken to the special care baby unit. Michelle sighed as the tiny girl was rushed away. She wouldn't trade her job because she enjoyed it too much.

The thought was in such stark contrast to how she'd felt the previous day that she frowned. Yesterday she'd wished she could walk away from all this, so what had changed? Was it the talk she'd had with Dominic that had made her feel so much better?

She sensed it was so and it worried her that he should have such a powerful effect on her emotions. When

Dominic left St Justin's in a few weeks' time she would have to get on with her life. The worst thing was knowing that nothing would ever be the same as it had been.

It was another half-hour before they finished in Resus. Lee Gerard had been sent to X-Ray and Sheryl was in the plaster room, having her fractures attended to. She would be transferred to the maternity unit after that.

The third patient had been sent to Theatre to have his ruptured spleen removed. The police were waiting to interview everyone concerned in the accident, but they would have to wait until the various treatments were completed. Michelle had no idea who was responsible for the accident because it wasn't her concern. Her job was to pick up the pieces afterwards.

She was on her way to Reception to make a start on whittling down the queue that had formed when Max waylaid her. He had another man with him and he drew the newcomer forward to introduce him.

'Michelle, I'd like you to meet Richard Hargreaves. He's thinking of applying for the trauma surgeon's post so he's come to have a look round.'

'Hello. Nice to meet you.' She smiled at the man. 'Max said that you've been working in the States?'

'That's right,' Richard agreed. He was in his mid-thirties with sandy blond hair and a pleasant face. Michelle was surprised when he suddenly frowned. 'Don't take this the wrong way, but I'm sure we've met somewhere before.'

'Have we?' She shrugged lightly because she didn't remember him. 'It's possible that we've bumped into one another at a lecture, I suppose.'

'Probably.' Richard agreed. He looked round when Max pointedly cleared his throat. 'I mustn't keep you because I can see that you're busy. It's nice to have met you, Michelle.'

'You, too,' she agreed pleasantly. She carried on to Reception and checked with Kate Morris, who was acting as triage nurse that day. 'Anything urgent?'

'Just one chap who I think you should take a look at.' Kate passed her the patient's notes then looked up and smiled as a shadow fell over them. 'Oh, look who's here. Some people lead a charmed life, swanning in at this hour of the day.'

Michelle felt her heart go bump as she looked up and saw Dominic standing in front of them. She heard him laugh at Kate's teasing and took a deep breath, but it did little to quell the feeling of excitement that was fizzing through her veins all of a sudden. It was an effort to respond calmly when he turned to her.

'Busy morning?'

'N-not really. We had an RTA, but apart from that it's been extremely quiet for once.'

She glanced at the notes she was holding then smiled at him, praying that he wouldn't suspect how shaken she felt. 'I'd better go check this one out.'

'There's nothing wrong, is there, Michelle?' he asked quietly as Kate moved away.

'Of course not. I'm just a bit abstracted. One of the patients from the RTA was pregnant and I delivered the baby,' she said quickly, hoping that he would accept that as the explanation. Frankly, she would find it difficult to come up with another one if he pressed her because she had no idea why she felt so on edge. Everything had been sorted out last night so why should she feel like this?

'Really? Wow! I think that calls for a celebration,' he declared, his green eyes sparkling with pleasure.

'What does?' Ruth put in, coming up behind them.

'Michelle just told me that she's delivered a baby and I think we should celebrate,' he explained.

'Sounds good to me,' Ruth agreed immediately. 'What were you thinking of?'

'How about a drink after work?' he suggested.

'Great.' Ruth turned to her. 'You will come, won't you, Michelle? I know you don't usually come out for a drink with us, but can't we persuade you just this once?'

Michelle didn't know what to say. Ruth would probably accept her refusal but how would Dominic feel about it? After all, he had gone to a lot of trouble last night.

'Say that you'll come, Michelle,' he said persuasively, his voice filled with something that made a shiver run through her. Maybe it was silly but she had the impression that it would mean a lot to him if she agreed.

'All right, then,' she said softly, feeling her pulse leap when she saw the pleasure that lit his eyes.

'Great.' He didn't get a chance to say anything else because Max came over at that point to introduce him to Richard Hargreaves.

Michelle took the opportunity to slip away, and for the rest of the afternoon she was careful to avoid any situation where she and Dominic might be left on their own.

She wasn't really sure why she didn't want to be alone with him. She just knew that she needed to keep busy and not think too much about what was going to happen that night. Not that it was a date, of course, when he had invited the whole department, but it was a big step for her to have taken after all this time. The funny thing was

how warm it made her feel inside to know that she
would never have taken it if it hadn't been for Dominic.

Dominic was a bundle of nerves as the hands on the
clock moved towards ten p.m. He found that he was
constantly watching the door, waiting for Michelle to
arrive. Quite a large party had gathered in the pub across
the street from the hospital. There were staff there from
a number of departments, as well as from A and E, and
he found himself hoping that it wouldn't all be too much
for Michelle. He would hate to think that she would find
it too overwhelming and would regret coming.

The door opened and he felt the blood rush to his head
when he saw her coming hesitantly into the bar. She
looked round uncertainly but before he had a chance to
get up and fetch her, Si Watson spotted her.

'Over here, Michelle,' the paramedic roared, standing
up and waving to her, thereby attracting everyone's attention.

Dominic bit back a groan when he saw the colour run
up her cheeks as everyone turned to look at her. For a
moment he thought that she was going to turn tail and
leave, then she squared her shoulders and headed towards them.

He got up as she approached their table and smiled at
her. 'That was some entrance.'

She laughed huskily as she slid into the seat. 'Not
intentional, I can assure you.' She looked round and
smiled as everyone said hello, but he could tell how
nervous she was.

'What would you like to drink?' he offered. 'It's my
round so you timed it just right.'

'Oh, a glass of white wine, please,' she replied, looking up at him.

Dominic drew in a quick breath but it was hard to control the hammering of his heart as he looked into her eyes and saw there a plea for reassurance. It touched him in a way he would never have expected to know that she was relying on him to help her through the ordeal.

'One glass of white wine coming up,' he said, letting his fingers rest lightly on her shoulder as he looked around the table. 'Same again, everyone?'

There was a chorus of assent from the rest of the party. Dominic gave her shoulder a last reassuring squeeze then went to the bar to order their drinks. Si went with him to help him carry them, chattering away about a football match he had watched on television. Dominic found it hard to concentrate when he kept wondering if Michelle would be OK, and if he had been right to persuade her to come with them that night. Should he have interfered in her life like that? Or should he have left things as they were?

His uncertainty lasted less than a second. There was no way he could have let her continue living the way she'd been doing for the past ten years!

They got the drinks at last and took them back to the table. He was relieved to see that she was chatting to Ruth and looked a lot more relaxed. He put the glass of wine on a coaster and pushed it towards her.

'Thanks.'

She treated him to a quick smile then returned to her conversation. Dominic sipped his own drink, letting the conversation flow around him. He didn't feel any need to join in because he was happy just watching Michelle coming out of her shell. She seemed to visibly gain confidence as the minutes passed, and when he heard her laugh he found himself smiling as well. It struck him all of a sudden just how much pleasure he could derive from knowing that she was happy. How strange.

They stayed in the pub until closing time. Dominic pushed back his chair as the barman rang the bell and asked everyone to drink up. 'Time we were off, I suppose.'

'I hadn't planned on staying this late,' Ruth declared, slipping her arms into her jacket. 'My husband will think I've got lost!'

'Tell him that you were abducted by aliens,' Si advised, grinning at her. 'It works for me every time.'

'Only because everybody is hoping that one day they won't bring you back,' Lisa retorted, making everyone laugh.

Dominic turned to Michelle as she rose. 'It wasn't too bad, I hope?'

'How did you guess...?' she began, then bit her lip.

'That you were scared stiff?' He smiled at her, curling his hands into fists because he ached to stop her doing such damage to her beautiful mouth. 'I could tell that the minute you walked in. It was a big step, Michelle, but now you've proved to yourself that there's nothing to be scared about, haven't you?'

'Yes.' She gave him a brilliant smile and he felt his heart rate increase to unprecedented levels when he saw the pleasure on her face. 'I know it must seem crazy to you, but I've got so used to being on my own outside work that I was terrified by the idea. But I've enjoyed it tonight, Dominic. It's been...well, fun. Thank you.'

She touched him lightly on the arm then turned when Ruth said something to her. Dominic made his way out of the pub in a daze. All that had happened had been that Michelle had touched his arm, but it felt as though a rocket had gone off inside him. It was an effort to get his thoughts together as everyone started saying their goodnights.

'Ruth's going to drop me off on her way home. She's got a taxi.'

He jumped when Michelle appeared at his side. 'Oh, I see. Fine.' He had been going to offer her a lift home because he'd been careful to stick to non-alcoholic beer all night. He felt a little spasm of disappointment run through him, but he knew that he couldn't let her see how he felt.

'I'll see you tomorrow, then, Dominic. Goodnight.'

She gave him a quick smile then hurried over to the waiting taxi and got in. Dominic waved as it sped away then made his way back to the hospital where he had left his car.

He started the engine then sat for a moment thinking about what had happened and how he felt, but it was hard to make sense of the jumble of emotions that seemed to be churning around inside him. All he knew was that being friends with Michelle was just as unsettling as being at odds with her.

CHAPTER EIGHT

THE time flew past and Michelle found it hard to keep track of the days. A couple of times she went to the pub after work with the rest of the staff, and she enjoyed the easy camaraderie, especially if Dominic was there.

He never tried to take over the conversation but he was amusing and informative, and so easy to get on with that she found it hard to believe her previous concerns about him. Maybe she wasn't one hundred per cent convinced that he'd done the right thing by opting out of hands-on medicine, but she was prepared to accept that *he* believed in what he did.

She attended Carmen's funeral and was touched when she saw that Dominic had sent flowers. The church was packed with the old lady's friends and it was such a happy occasion that nobody went away feeling sad after it was over. Carmen had asked that everyone wear bright colours instead of black, so the congregation was suitably clad for the occasion, and Michelle felt quite drab in her sober grey suit and white blouse.

She was on nights all weekend because the agency had finally found someone to cover, but only through the daytime. She went into work at six and was surprised to discover that there had been a change made to the filming schedule. Dominic had decided that he needed some film of what happened in the department during the night, and especially at the weekend when they were always busy. Max had left her a note, informing her of the changes, and she had just read it when Dominic tapped on the office door.

'I hope you don't mind this switch to nights instead of days,' he said, coming into the room. 'I think it's important that we emphasise that working in A and E is a twenty-four-hour-a-day job.'

'It's fine by me,' she said immediately. 'It's usually a bit hectic on weekends, though. We get a lot of trouble when the clubs let out around three in the morning.'

'Nothing changes,' he said ruefully, coming over to perch on the edge of the desk. 'Fridays and Saturdays were always the two worst nights when I worked in A and E.'

Michelle felt a little shiver run through her when he smiled at her. He was sitting so close that she could see the tiny crinkles at the corners of his eyes. As usual he was casually dressed in a white shirt and navy-blue trousers, but the clothes fitted him to perfection, emphasising his broad shoulders and muscular chest, the length of his powerful legs.

Dominic Walsh was an extremely attractive man and she couldn't help noticing that, even though she didn't want to be aware of such things. She could cope with the thought of him being her friend but she couldn't deal with the idea of him being more than that.

Not yet.

She flushed as the thought slid into her mind and saw him frown. 'Is something wrong?'

'Of course not,' she said quickly. She picked up another of the notes that Max had left for her. 'That fellow who came to look round the other day has applied for the trauma post.'

'That should ease things a bit,' he said evenly, but she

could see the curiosity that lingered in his eyes and knew that he hadn't believed her.

'It should.' She searched for something else to say to ease the tension that seemed to have sprung up between them. She didn't want anything more than friendship from Dominic; she didn't! 'When is your next show being broadcast?'

'Tonight, as it happens.' He stood up abruptly and went to the window, and she saw him run a hand through his hair in a gesture that spoke of impatience—but impatience about what exactly? Had she done something to upset him?

'It's scheduled for eight o'clock so maybe you'll get a chance to watch it if you aren't too busy.'

She blinked when she realised that he was speaking to her. 'Hopefully. I would like to see it.'

'Really? You aren't just saying that to humour me?'

She smiled when she heard the scepticism in his voice, feeling a little of her tension disappear. What on earth was the matter with her? Why was she looking for problems that didn't exist?

'No, I'm not. I really am interested to see what you've made of us all.'

'I've tried to portray everyone exactly as they are,' he stated firmly. 'I insisted that Hugh let me take charge of the editing for that very reason.'

'So you managed to talk him out of the buckets-of-gore scenario he was planning?'

He laughed deeply. 'Too right! You don't need to hike up the drama because there's more than enough in any A and E department. It comes with the territory.'

He looked round when the cameraman knocked on the door to tell him that there was a phone call for him.

'Probably Hugh, having a last-minute panic because I'm not there. I'd better go.'

She smiled as he hurried away. Funnily enough, she was looking forward to seeing the programme despite her earlier misgivings. She knew that Dominic would do as he had promised and show life in the department exactly as it was.

It brought it home to her all over again how wrong she had been about him. Still, they had cleared up their misunderstandings and he seemed to have forgiven her for the way she'd behaved initially. It was good to know that she could trust him completely. She hadn't felt like this about anyone except Stephen.

The thought sent a little shock through her and she shivered. Stephen had been her husband, the man she had loved, and it didn't seem right to compare Dominic to him. It opened up the way for other comparisons and that was something she couldn't allow to happen. Nothing must ever detract from Stephen's memory!

She tried to conjure up his image but it just wouldn't seem to form in her mind. It was like a shadow floating in the background, hazy and indistinct. Once she'd only needed to shut her eyes and she'd been able to see him, but now it felt as though he was just beyond her reach.

She felt her eyes sting with tears. Was it just the passage of time that was taking Stephen away from her, or was it because she was thinking about someone else, about Dominic? The idea that he might be replacing Stephen in her thoughts was almost more than she could bear because it seemed like the worst kind of betrayal.

The evening was fairly steady. Michelle was relieved that she was kept busy because it meant that she had no time to brood. They had a bit of a flurry around seven o'clock when an injured motorcyclist was rushed in. They did their best but his injuries were so severe that he didn't survive.

Michelle dealt with the harrowing task of informing his family, a job she always hated yet one which had to be done. He was only nineteen and his parents were distraught.

She stayed with them for some time then left them to sit with their son. When she left Resus the department was deserted. There was just Trisha sitting behind the reception desk and nobody waiting to be seen.

'Where is everyone?' she asked in amazement.

'In the staffroom, watching *Health Matters*.' Trisha sighed. 'I've got my sister recording it for me so I'll have to wait till I get home to see if I've been turned into a superstar.'

Michelle laughed. 'I hope you aren't thinking of giving up your job on the strength of your performance because we'd hate to lose you. Anyway, I'll go and have a peek. Give me a shout if you need me.'

She made her way to the staffroom and grinned when she found most of the staff packed in there. 'It's like the *Marie Celeste* out there.'

'That's because the punters are all watching the show,' Bryan Patterson declared, moving over so that she could sit on the arm of his chair.

The opening credits suddenly appeared on the screen and everyone stopped talking. Michelle felt her heart jolt when Dominic appeared on camera. He was dressed much as he had been the first time she'd seen him, in an expensive jacket and tailored trousers, but now she could see past the polished exterior to the man beneath. A feeling of warmth filled her as he smiled at the camera because it felt as though he was smiling directly at her...

She shrugged off that silly idea, hearing the gasps and laughter as various people saw themselves on television. She seemed to feature quite prominently in the film, something which the others weren't slow to remark on when it was over.

'I'm jealous!' Helen Andrews teased her. 'You certainly had a starring role in the programme, Michelle.'

'Didn't she just? And there was poor old Max, worrying himself to death in case the camera showed up his bald patch,' Sandra Hunt put in. 'He needn't have bothered because we only caught the odd glimpse of him when Michelle wasn't around!'

'It was just the luck of the draw,' she said, blushing when everyone hooted in derision.

'Oh, she's so innocent it makes you weep, doesn't it?' Bryan gave her a friendly hug. 'The fact that you played the leading role had nothing whatsoever to do with the fact that Dominic just happens to fancy you rotten?'

'Don't be ridiculous!' she exclaimed, feeling her heart thundering away. Dominic attracted to her? Oh, surely not?

'There's nothing at all ridiculous about it,' Bryan said cheerily. 'But being the kind-hearted soul that I am, I'll spare your blushes.' He looked at the others and winked. 'We know what's been going on around here, though.'

'Well, you obviously know more than I do,' she said hotly.

Michelle quickly made her way to the door and nothing more was said. However, that didn't mean she could forget about it. The idea that Dominic was interested in her that way should have made her laugh but, oddly enough, it didn't. Try as she would, she couldn't stop the feeling of excitement that invaded her at the thought of him finding her attractive. It had been a long time since she'd felt like that—a very long time indeed.

It took Dominic some time to get away from the studio. There was the usual post-broadcast discussion, although everyone was agreed that the programme had been one of the best they had ever produced. The report about the abandoned baby had touched a lot of viewers and the phones had been kept busy with people ringing in to say how much they'd enjoyed hearing an update on his progress.

More calls were coming in to say how much people had enjoyed seeing a realistic portrayal of the work that was done in the A and E department, and Michelle's name featured heavily in the tributes that were paid to the staff. A lot of viewers had been struck by her expertise and dedication, and it warmed his heart to know that people had noticed what a very special person she was.

He finally made it to St Justin's at a little before eleven and hurried into Reception to find a queue of people waiting to be seen. Trisha greeted him with surprise.

'We didn't know you were coming back tonight, Dominic. I thought the cameraman was just going to stay here and film.'

'I told Max that I intended to come back. He must have forgotten to mention it.' He glanced over his shoulder then grinned at Trisha. 'Of course, I can always leave if I'm not wanted.'

'Don't you dare!' she said quickly. 'I'll be hung, drawn and quartered if the others discovered that I'd let you escape when we've got a queue.'

'Is it just Michelle on tonight?' he asked, thinking that

the staff were going to have their work cut out, dealing with the amount of people who needed attending to.

'John's working as well, and Sandra Hunt, our nurse practitioner. She can deal with the cuts and bruises, dislocated ankles, and so on,' Trisha explained. 'It takes a bit of pressure off Michelle and John to have her here.'

'And hopefully I can take some more pressure off them. Just give me a few minutes to put my jacket away and I'll be right with you.'

He hurriedly made his way to the locker room, pausing when he spotted Michelle coming out of one of the cubicles. She had a youth with her who had a heavy lint pad strapped over his left eye. He waited until she'd finished explaining to the patient that he would need to visit the outpatients department the following day then went over to her.

'Hi, there.'

'Dominic!'

He saw the surprise on her face and knew that she hadn't been expecting him to make it back after the show either. However, it wasn't that which intrigued him but the way the colour suddenly came rushing to her cheeks. He found himself wondering what had caused her to react like that but, short of asking her, he had no way of knowing.

'I did warn you I would be working tonight,' he reminded her lightly, determined not to let her see how mixed up he felt all of a sudden. The fact that Michelle seemed to be so aware of him was doing strange things to his equilibrium. It made him even more aware of her than he normally was so that it was an effort to control the jolt his pulse gave when she stepped aside to let someone pass and the side of her breast brushed his arm.

'Yes, of course.'

She moved away again and he could see that her colour had deepened. That it was the contact between them that had caused it to happen wasn't in any doubt, and his racing pulse seemed to go into overdrive. He had to clear his throat before he could say anything and even then his voice sounded rather strangled when it emerged.

'Perhaps I should have phoned to remind you. Sorry.'

'Don't be silly,' she said quickly, but he could see the shock that had lit her grey eyes. 'We're just glad to have you here to help. I did see the show tonight, by the way. It was very good. That part about the baby was really touching.'

He felt a sudden elation fill him at the praise. 'I'm really pleased, Michelle. It means a lot to me to know that you enjoyed it.'

'I did.'

She looked up and he saw a smile light her beautiful face. 'I think I understand now what you're trying to do, Dominic. Educating people about their health is vital.'

'I am so glad.' He took her hands and held them as a wave of joy washed over him. Frankly, he couldn't believe how pleased he was to hear such a positive opinion from her.

'I...I'd better get on,' she said quietly, quickly withdrawing her hands.

'And I'd better put my jacket away before Trisha thinks I've run out on her. There's quite a queue in the waiting room,' he explained when she looked at him quizzically. 'I promised her that I wouldn't be long.'

'Typical Friday night,' she said lightly.

She moved away to attend to a patient Amy had just brought through. Dominic went to put his jacket in a locker then returned to Reception. Trisha was speaking to a woman at the counter and she beckoned him over.

'Can you have a word with this lady, please, Dominic?' she said quietly. 'I wasn't really sure what to say to her, to be honest.'

'What's it about?' he asked, frowning as he glanced at the woman.

'It's something to do with that baby who was abandoned. Evidently, she saw your show tonight and that's why she came.' Trisha shrugged. 'I told her that she needed to speak to the police but she said that she wanted to speak to you.'

'Fine. I'll take her into the relatives' room,' he said, quickly making up his mind. 'Did you get her name, by the way?'

'No, she wouldn't give it to me.' Trisha went to answer the phone, obviously relieved to be able to hand over the problem.

Dominic went over to the woman and smiled at her. She was Asian, in her late twenties, and very attractive. 'Hello, I'm Dominic Walsh. I believe you wanted to have a word with me. Maybe you'd like to come into the relatives' room so we can speak in private?'

He led the way, closing the door and turning over the sign to show that the room was occupied. He gestured towards one of the chairs. 'Please, sit down, Miss...'

'Kumar, Meena Kumar.' She took a seat then looked at him and he could see the worry in her eyes. 'Did the receptionist explain why I'm here?'

'She said that it had something to do with the abandoned baby.' He looked questioningly at her after he had sat down. 'Do you have some information?'

'I'm not sure. I'm not even sure what I'm doing here. It's just that I had this feeling, you understand...'

She broke off and swallowed. Dominic gave her a moment to collect herself. 'If you can tell us anything

at all, it would be a great help. We really have very little
to go on at the moment. The baby's mother has refused
to tell us her name so we haven't been able to contact
her family.'

'I think she might be my sister, Sunita,' she said hesitantly.

'And why do you think that?'

'Because she's missing from home and a neighbour
told me that she had seen Sunita knocking on my door
while I was away.' She shook her head. 'It sounds so
silly, but I sensed there was something wrong with Sunita the last time I saw her, about four months ago. My
family lives in Leicester and I don't get a chance to see
them very often because of my work.'

'What do you do?' he put in, trying to curb the excitement he felt. It would be wonderful for everyone
involved if they could find out the girl's identity.

'I'm a flight attendant,' she told him. 'I do long-haul
trips—Australia, the Philippines, Japan. I flew out to
Australia two weeks ago and stayed over for a holiday.
My fiancé lives in Sydney, you see.'

'And you think that your sister—Sunita, was it? You
think Sunita came to see you while you were away?'

'Yes. When I got home last night there were messages
on my answering machine from my parents, telling me
that Sunita was missing. They have tried all her friends
but nobody knows where she's gone.' She took a deep
breath but he could tell how difficult she was finding it
to talk about her sister.

'And you think that Sunita might have run away from
home because she was pregnant?' he prompted gently.

'Yes. She would be scared out of her mind and
wouldn't know what to do. She's only sixteen and she's
always been very sheltered.' She sighed. 'It's a huge

disgrace in Asian circles when something like this happens, you understand?'

'So she probably thought that you would be the best person to help her?' he suggested thoughtfully.

'Oh, yes. I just wish she'd told me what was going on then I could have done something sooner. You said in your report tonight that the baby's mother was found in an alley?'

'That's right. She must have delivered the baby herself because we found him in some public toilets close to where she was found.'

'Oh!' Meena put her hand over her mouth. 'I can't bear to think what might have happened to her.'

'We still have to check if she is your sister,' he warned her, getting up. 'I'll phone the ward and ask if you can see her. I know it's late but it would be best if this was sorted out as soon as possible.'

He made the call then escorted Meena upstairs once he had permission from the nurse on duty. She met them outside the ward and took Meena to the side room where the baby's mother had been staying since her admission.

Dominic paced the floor, hoping that the mystery had been solved at last. When the ward nurse came back and quietly informed him that it was indeed Meena's sister, Sunita Kumar, he breathed a sigh of relief.

He went back to A and E, intending to find Michelle and tell her the good news, but there was pandemonium in the A and E department. A fight had broken out between rival groups of youths in a nearby club and several of them had been injured. The fact that they seemed intent on continuing their scrap in the middle of the hospital was causing chaos.

'I've asked Security to send some more men to deal

with this,' Michelle told him on her way to treat a boy with a knife wound down his cheek.

'Let's hope they hurry up,' he said drily, making a grab for a second youth who was about to aim a punch at the first one. 'Oh, no, you don't. If you want to be treated, you settle yourself down.'

He glanced round when he heard Michelle laugh, feeling a ripple run down his spine when he saw the way she was looking at him.

'I know who to call if I need a hand,' she said lightly, but the words didn't feel at all light when he heard them.

'Any time and any place. You only have to shout and I'll be there, Michelle.'

She didn't say anything to that but he knew that she'd understood what he'd meant. It scared him in a way because it was a situation he hadn't been in before. He wanted to be there for her for always and ever; he would happily spend his life taking care of her if she would let him.

He felt a sudden pain pierce his heart and turned away, ostensibly to lead the youth into a cubicle only he knew that it was so she wouldn't guess how he felt. He ordered the boy to remove his shirt so that he could examine the knife wound he had received to his upper arm. It was a clean cut and not very deep, but it would require stitching so he asked Amy to set everything up.

He gave the youth a shot of local anaesthetic and cleaned the wound then set to work. However, the whole time he was carefully drawing together the edges of the wound he found that he was having to force himself to concentrate. His mind was full of the thought that he could never replace Stephen in Michelle's heart, and it hurt. It hurt a lot.

*   *   *

They worked steadily until just after midnight when there was a lull. Michelle sent Sandra and Amy for their meal breaks, and told John to take a breather. Dominic was attending to an old lady who had fallen down the stairs so she went to see if he needed a hand.

She paused outside the cubicle when she heard the old lady, Agnes Hilliard, laugh at something he said to her. He was so good with all the patients, young and old, immediately knowing how to put them at their ease. It was a gift that not all doctors possessed but Dominic's ability to relate to people was one of the things about him that impressed her most.

She sighed as she pushed aside the curtain. It wasn't the only thing that had impressed her. The list was growing by the day. Coming on top of what Bryan had told her that night about Dominic fancying her, it was deeply unsettling. She liked Dominic and admired him. That would be fine if she didn't have to add the next bit. She was also attracted to him and it was that which worried her most because of its implications.

'I've nearly finished here. I was just telling Mrs Hilliard that I wished all our patients were as well behaved as her.'

Michelle summoned a smile when he turned to her, knowing that it would be unwise to let him see how confused she felt. 'So she's not been causing you too much bother?' she said lightly, smiling at the old lady.

'She's been a model patient—quiet and respectful, *and* she laughs at my jokes. What more could any doctor ask for?'

He treated the old lady to a wonderfully warm smile. 'There will be someone down shortly from Orthopaedics to see you. I'm afraid your hip will need operating on but they can do marvellous things nowadays. Just try to rest and I'll be back soon to check on you.'

Michelle led the way from the cubicle, pausing while he drew the curtains across to give the old lady some privacy. 'We seem to have quietened down a bit so I wondered if you wanted to take your break?'

'I'll leave it until I've made sure that Mrs Hilliard is all right. She's been very brave but it's been a shock for her and I'd like to stay here until she goes to Theatre.' He looked at her questioningly. 'Is that OK?'

'Of course it is! You don't need to ask my permission. I'm just glad to have your help. We wouldn't have managed half so well tonight without you.'

'Oh, more, please! It does wonders for my ego to hear you say that,' he teased.

Michelle laughed, feeling her heart turn over when she caught the full force of his smile. He was devastating when he smiled like that. His whole face seemed to light up, his eyes filling with a warmth that made her want to bask in it and let it wash away all her problems.

'I don't think your ego needs any bolstering,' she replied, but even she could hear the husky note that had crept into her voice.

'Maybe not, but it's good to hear you say nice things about me, Michelle,' he said softly.

They were standing in the corridor by the cubicles and there was nobody about. When he stepped towards her and placed his hands lightly on her shoulders, she didn't move.

'I could get used to it.'

Michelle knew he was going to kiss her. She could see it in his eyes, feel it in her heart, but she made no attempt to stop what was happening for the simple reason that she didn't want to.

His lips brushed lightly over hers, so softly and delicately that she shivered. His hands tightened as he drew her towards him and let his mouth settle more firmly over hers so that she could feel its shape and taste its sweetness. She gave a soft moan and felt him grow tense before he suddenly set her away from him.

'I shouldn't have done that. I apologise.'

She took a wobbly breath as she realised that he'd misinterpreted her moan of pleasure for one of dismay. 'There's no need to apologise.'

'Isn't there?' He smiled but his eyes were full of remorse all of a sudden.

'No, of course not,' she said quickly, feeling a little sick. Dominic obviously regretted having kissed her and it hurt to know that. It was a relief when the sound of laughter heralded the return of Sandra and Amy back from their breaks.

Michelle told them that she would take her meal break and fled to the canteen. She made herself eat the rather dry sandwiches that were the only food available at that time of the night, although she wasn't really hungry— or at least not for food.

She closed her eyes, remembering how Dominic's lips had felt, how sweet and gentle they had been. It wasn't food she needed to satiate this hunger, she realised sickly. She wanted Dominic to kiss her again, to take her in his arms and hold her, to fill her body with the feel and scent and taste of his. She wanted him to make love to her and the thought was unbearably painful because it was a betrayal of everything she had felt for Stephen.

How could she want another man this way? Why did she ache to feel Dominic's arms around her when up till now she'd been perfectly content with her celibate existence?

Yet no matter how hard she tried she couldn't rid herself of the hunger that had awoken inside her. What scared her most of all was that she might not have the strength to fight her feelings in the future.

The night drew on, becoming busy again once the clubs closed. It never failed to amaze Michelle what people did to themselves in the name of enjoyment, but dealing with the aftermath was all part of the job. At least it meant that she didn't have time to dwell on what had happened with Dominic, and how it had made her feel.

It was almost four when they had a call from Ambulance Control to say that they would be receiving two burn victims. St Justin's had a dedicated burn unit so she alerted the on-call registrar then called everyone together.

'We have a mother and a young child on their way in. They've been involved in a house fire. I'm not sure what degree of burns they both have but we'll need to adopt a strictly sterile policy when treating them.'

She broke off as Trisha called her over to answer another call from Ambulance Control, feeling her heart sink when she heard the new message.

'What's happened?' Dominic asked quickly when she went back.

'Someone has thrown a brick through the ambulance windscreen. Lisa has been hurt and they're having to send out another ambulance to ferry her and Si here, as well as the two patients we were expecting.'

'Did they say how bad Lisa was?' Sandra asked worriedly.

'No. We'll have to wait and see when she gets here.'

She heard Dominic swear under his breath and grimaced. 'I know. It seems unbelievable that anyone would do a thing like that, but it's happened before.'

'I'm going to get Mike to film this,' he said tersely. 'The public needs to be made aware of what people like Lisa have to put up with.'

She frowned as she watched him go over to the cameraman. It affected them all when something like this happened. However, she couldn't help wondering if his anger had been genuine. He seemed to have rallied quickly enough because he was now going through the shots he wanted Mike Soames to take when Lisa arrived. It made her wonder all of a sudden if she could trust him, then she realised what she was doing. She was looking for a reason to dislike him because she couldn't handle how she *really* felt.

The ambulances started to arrive just then fortunately, so she put that disquieting thought to the back of her mind as she went out to meet them. The burns registrar had arrived and he went into Resus with them. The mother had second-degree burns to her legs and lower body, caused when she'd carried her daughter down the stairs through the flames. She'd had the presence of mind to wrap the child in a wet towel so, apart from some minor burns to the little girl's left foot, she wasn't too badly injured.

Michelle left the registrar to deal with them and went to the door as Lisa was wheeled in. She could barely hide her dismay when she saw the damage that had been done to the paramedic's face. Si had accompanied her in the ambulance and he was obviously deeply shocked by what had happened.

'There was nothing I could do,' he kept saying over and over again.

Michelle glanced at Sandra, who quickly came over and led him out, leaving her free to deal with Lisa. She bent over the young paramedic and smiled at her. 'Some night, eh?'

Lisa nodded because she couldn't speak. The brick had come straight through the windscreen of the ambulance and smashed into the right side of her face. Her right eye was swollen shut and her ear and cheek were horribly bruised. Some of her teeth had come out and she was having a lot of trouble with her gums bleeding.

Michelle gently felt along Lisa's lower jawbone and felt her wince. It was obviously broken, possibly in more than one place. She checked the left side of the paramedic's lower jaw because quite often the side opposite to the one that had received the blow turned out to be fractured as well, but she couldn't detect any breaks in it.

'Hey, how are you doing?'

Dominic came over and crouched in front of Lisa. He tilted his head and studied her swollen face. 'So what does the other guy look like?'

Lisa's good eye filled with tears and he gripped her hand. 'It will be all right, sweetheart. We'll soon get you sorted out and back to looking beautiful again, won't we, Michelle?'

He looked up and she felt a little river of warmth flow through her when she saw the concern in his eyes. It was obvious that it hadn't been an act before and that he was genuinely worried.

'Of course we will,' she said swiftly, feeling her heart lift. With Dominic's help they got Lisa onto the bed and quickly started to clean up some of the blood. The girl was shivering with shock so they covered her with a blanket and Michelle decided to set up a drip because she had lost quite a lot of blood. Painkillers took the edge off Lisa's discomfort while they waited to hear when she could be sent to Theatre. It was a relief for them all when the call came through that everything was ready.

Michelle accompanied her from Resus, pausing *en route* to the lift when Si came hurrying over. 'Hang in there, kiddo,' he said, bending down to look at her. 'I just wish it had been me driving.'

Lisa pointed to the pen Michelle was holding. She gave it to her, along with the back of the admission form she had just filled in. Everyone laughed when Si read aloud what Lisa had written. '"I wish you'd been driving as well!"'

Si insisted on going up to Theatre with them and Michelle didn't have the heart to refuse. He was still very shocked but she knew that he needed to reassure himself that Lisa would be all right.

They handed her over to the anaesthetist then went back downstairs to A and E where Si finally agreed to let Sandra take him into the staffroom and make him a cup of tea. The police had arrived and they went with him to take a statement and by then it was time for her to go home. She handed over to the young registrar supplied by the agency with a feeling of relief. It had been quite a night one way and another.

She collected her jacket and said goodbye to the others. It was a beautiful morning, the sun casting a delicate lemon haze over the sky. The air smelt so sweet and clean at that time of the day, before the morning rush hour got under way. It seemed a shame to go home to bed, but where else could she go?

'What a night that was.'

She looked round when Dominic joined her on the

step, feeling her heart giving that increasingly familiar little flutter. 'Sorry you stayed?'

'Not at all. I wouldn't have missed it for a moment, although I would love to be able to rewrite the script in places.'

'You mean Lisa getting hurt?'

'How did you guess?' he said in surprise.

How indeed? She shrugged, not wanting to make too much out of the fact that she'd known what he was thinking.

'Lucky guess. Anyhow, I'd better go home and get some sleep.'

'I don't know if I'll be able to sleep,' he admitted, walking with her along the drive. 'My mind feels far too active, to be honest.'

'I know what you mean,' she said. 'It takes me ages to unwind after a turn on nights.'

'Then how about making the most of this beautiful morning, rather than rushing straight home to bed?' He turned to her and she couldn't fail to see the plea in his eyes.

'What did you have in mind?' she said slowly, wondering if she was mad to ask such a question. Surely it would be playing with fire to spend more time with Dominic, but she couldn't deny that the thought was too tempting to resist.

'A drive to the river. It's absolutely magical at this time of day.' He touched her hand lightly, with the very tips of his fingers, yet it felt as though her blood were suddenly on fire. 'Say you'll come, Michelle. Please.'

CHAPTER NINE

TRAFFIC was light as they drove out of the city. Although the morning rush hour was starting, most of the vehicles were heading in the opposite direction.

Dominic slipped a CD into the stereo and turned down the volume so that the music provided a pleasant background while they drove. Michelle had her eyes closed and her head was resting against the back of her seat, but he didn't think she was asleep. There was far too much tension in the air for her to sleep through it.

He took a deep breath as it struck him that he might have made a big mistake by inviting her to go with him. He wasn't sure what he'd hoped to achieve other than the pleasure of her company for a while longer. However, he couldn't ignore the fact that he might be playing with fire.

He was too aware of Michelle and how she made him feel to risk spending time alone with her and not show how he felt. He only had to recall her murmur of dismay when he'd kissed her earlier to know that it would be a mistake to give in to his urges. She was still in love with her husband. If he repeated that over and over, surely it would make him see sense?

'That's nice. What is it?'

He jumped when she spoke, not understanding at first what she meant before he realised she had been referring to the music. 'A Bryan Adams track. I went to a concert of his last year and bought it there.'

'So you're a rock fan?'

He heard the surprise in her voice and laughed. 'Yes. Why, does that surprise you?'

'I'm not sure...' She pursed her lips as she considered her answer, and he bit back a groan when he saw her beautiful lips pucker so invitingly. It was an effort to act as though there was nothing wrong when she suddenly smiled at him.

'It just doesn't fit your image, I suppose.'

'You mean that you had me summed up as someone who enjoys classical music of the heavier kind?' He shook his head when she raised her brows. 'Sorry to disappoint you. My musical tastes are more low-brow than high-brow.'

'I'm not disappointed, just intrigued.' She turned sideways in the seat and regarded him thoughtfully. 'So, what else do you like listening to as well as rock?'

'Blues, jazz, pop.' He felt his heart lurch when she grinned at him.

'How about country and western? You've more or less covered everything else.'

'I have been known to listen to the odd tape or two.' He pretended to glare at her when she laughed. 'There's some really great music put out under the heading of country and western, I'll have you know!'

'Oh, I'm sure there is. It just strikes me as funny that the sophisticated Dr Dominic Walsh enjoys it, that's all.'

'I'm not sure if that's an insult or a compliment so I'll refrain from replying,' he declared, turning off the high street. He drove up the road then parked in front of his house and switched off the engine.

'I thought we could leave the car here and walk to the river. It's only a few minutes away.'

'Fine by me.' She got out and stretched luxuriously. 'Oh, it does feel good to be out in the fresh air!'

He locked the car then came round to join her. 'Nice not to smell antiseptic for a change?'

'Too right!' She took another huge lungful then looked around. 'This is a lovely area. These houses must be beautiful inside.'

'Want to take a look?' he suggested, jangling his keys.

'You mean you live here?' she exclaimed.

Dominic frowned, not sure what had prompted that sudden note of alarm in her voice. 'That's right. This is my house. I moved here last year. I felt it was time I took the plunge and bought my own place rather than renting as I had been doing.'

He knew he was talking too fast but he felt uncomfortable with her reaction, even more so when he saw her glance uncertainly at the house.

'I had no idea you intended bringing me to your house.'

He felt his heart sink as he realised what must be going through her mind. 'I brought you to the river, Michelle. The fact that I happen to live nearby is just a coincidence, but if you feel uncomfortable about being here I'll take you home.'

He turned to unlock the car then stopped when she put her hand on his arm. 'No, don't do that. I...I want to stay.'

She took a quick breath and he saw a little colour wash up her face. 'It's too nice a morning to miss out on such a treat.'

He smiled at her, hoping that it would reassure her. She was as nervous as a kitten around him and that didn't make the situation any easier when it made him wonder why she reacted that way.

'It is. Let's go and walk along the riverbank then we

can stop for breakfast at a little café I know. They make the most wonderful fresh croissants.'

'Sounds like fun,' she agreed softly.

They walked up the road side by side. It was a little after seven and there were a number of people about. Dominic led the way along the path to the river, putting a hand under her elbow to guide her out of the way when a jogger came racing up behind them and tried to get past.

'I wish I had some of his energy,' she said ruefully, staring after the man as he pounded up the path ahead of them.

'You don't really,' he assured her. 'If you were racing along like that, you wouldn't have time to enjoy the day.'

'No, I suppose not. Oh, how lovely!' They had reached the river by that point and she stopped to take in the view.

'Oh, look!' she exclaimed, pointing to a pair of swans that were swimming close to the far bank. 'Aren't they beautiful?'

'There are a lot of swans this year,' he told her, enjoying her delight in the scene. 'Most of them have nested so we might see some cygnets if we're lucky.'

'I wish I'd brought some bread with me,' she declared, then laughed self-consciously. 'You must think I'm mad, wanting to feed the swans at my age.'

'I think no such thing,' he assured her firmly. 'In fact, I often bring a bag of bread down here to feed the swans and the ducks.'

'Really?' She looked at him with huge grey eyes that had turned misty all of a sudden. 'Stephen and I used to go to Regent's Park and feed the ducks there. We never had much money to spare but it didn't seem to matter when we enjoyed doing simple things like that.'

'It's who you do things with that matters most,' he said quietly, struggling to contain the pain that had knifed through him. Listening to her talking about the other man was difficult because it was a sharp reminder that Stephen played a pivotal role in her life even now.

'That's very true. A lot of people believe that you need to spend money to have a good time, but you don't. A walk in the park can be more wonderful than a night out at an expensive restaurant as long as you're with the right person.'

The wistfulness in her voice cut him to the quick and he cleared his throat, afraid that she would guess how painful he was finding the conversation. 'I certainly won't argue with that sentiment. So, shall we stroll along the riverbank? I don't know about you but I could do with a little gentle exercise, and the emphasis is on the word ''gentle'', I hasten to add.'

She laughed at that and he breathed a sigh of relief when he saw the shadows fade from her eyes. 'I'd love a walk, thank you. And I promise we can go as slowly as you want to.'

He groaned. 'That makes me feel like some poor old crock. At this rate I'll have to break the habits of a lifetime and take up jogging!'

'It might be a good idea,' she said with a completely deadpan expression. 'It would stop you getting flabby.'

'Flabby? Flabby! How dare you, you wretched woman? It's a good job there are so many witnesses about otherwise you might find yourself in that water.'

She laughed joyously, her whole face lighting up. 'Just try it. Go on—I dare you!'

Dominic held up his hands in a gesture of appeasement. 'OK, I was only teasing. Now, come along. The morning is awasting, as the Bard would say.'

He held out his hand, feeling a rush of pleasure hit his system when Michelle immediately slid hers into it. He took a steadying breath as they set off along the riverbank, but his blood was racing and his pulse was almost out of control. Holding hands with Michelle was the cause of it and it shocked him on one level to know that anything so innocent could create such a flood of sexual awareness. On another level, however, it seemed perfectly understandable.

Michelle meant more to him than any other woman had. She touched him in ways he had never expected, made him feel things that would have been alien a couple of weeks ago. He was falling in love with her, slowly but inevitably, and there wasn't a thing he could do about it. That she might never be able to love him in return was something he refused to think about. He would simply enjoy this magical, wonderful morning and let the future take care of itself.

They must have walked several miles along the riverbank. It was so peaceful by the water that she guessed Dominic was as loath as she was to turn back. They didn't talk very much because they were both content just to enjoy the peace and quiet after the bustle of the busy night. They reached the café he had told her about and stopped.

'Coffee and croissants still sound good to you?'

'Perfect,' she agreed, trying to recall when she'd last enjoyed herself so much.

'How about sitting out here, then?' He pointed to one of the small iron tables arranged outside the café and she nodded.

'Even more perfect.'

'I'm not sure that's grammatically correct but I know what you mean.' He gave her a warm smile then went into the café.

Michelle walked over to a table and pulled out one of the iron chairs. It was soaked with dew so she found a tissue in her pocket and dried the seat before sitting down. There was a cluster of swans preening their feathers near to the bank and she watched them, entranced by their gracefulness. Dominic came back with their breakfast, hooking out a chair and sitting down before she had a chance to warn him about the seats being wet. She heard him groan as the dew immediately soaked through his trousers.

'I'm sopping wet,' he exclaimed, standing up again so that she could see the wet patch on the seat of his trousers.

'I should have warned you. Sorry!'

She tried to hide her amusement and failed miserably when a giggle escaped her. He treated her to a baleful stare as he sat down again.

'Think it's funny that I'll have to walk back with a soaking wet backside and everyone will think that I've wet myself?'

'No, of course not,' she began, then doubled up with laughter. 'I'm *so* sorry but it really is funny.'

'Don't forget what I threatened before, Dr Roberts. You're still rather too close to that water to take any risks,' he growled, trying to sound menacing and failing miserably.

Michelle wiped her eyes with the back of her hand and tried to sober up. 'I won't make fun of you again—promise. Shall I pour the coffee?'

She picked up the pot and filled two giant white cups

with the steaming brew. There was a plate of buttery croissants as well as a dish of home-made strawberry jam to go with them, so she helped herself.

Breaking off an end of the warm pastry, she daubed it with jam then popped it into her mouth and sighed with pleasure. 'Mmm, that is just so delicious.'

'The chef is French and he has the flour sent over specially from his home town,' he informed her, as he liberally spread jam onto a piece of roll. They ate in silence, refilling their cups with coffee until every scrap and drop had been eaten and drunk.

Michelle sat back and gave a deep sigh. 'To think I would have gone straight home if you hadn't invited me to come with you, and missed all this.'

'So you feel better for being here?' he asked softly, yet with a grating note in his voice that made her look at him curiously.

'Yes, of course. Why?'

'No reason.' Dominic shrugged but she could tell that he was trying to avoid answering her question as he got up to take the tray back into the café.

She got up, wondering why the blood seemed to be flowing a little faster through her veins all of a sudden. Was it because she sensed that it had been important to him that she should have enjoyed herself that morning— enjoyed being with *him*?

It was an effort to respond even though he kept up an undemanding conversation as they made their way back along the riverbank. They walked up the road to where he had left his car, and she stopped when he hesitated. 'Is something wrong?'

'Would you mind if we stopped off at my house while I change out of these wet trousers?' He grimaced. 'I don't fancy the thought of having to drive back to the city in this state.'

'Would you like me to wait in the car?' she suggested, feeling her heart starting to pound.

'If you want to,' he said easily, making her feel a bit of a fool for even suggesting that she should wait outside.

'I'll come in, then,' she said firmly. 'I'd love to have a look around while you get changed.'

'Be my guest.' He unlocked the front door and quickly deactivated the alarm before ushering her inside a long, narrow hallway. 'The living room is the first door on your right, dining room behind it and the kitchen at the end of the hall. Go and explore while I get changed.'

He loped off up the stairs, leaving her to make her way into the living room. She paused in the doorway and took stock. Dominic's style was surprisingly informal, although he'd taken care to keep everything in harmony with the age of the house.

The floor was the original wooden boards, stripped and buffed to a soft sheen. A large rug in front of the fireplace in varying shades of green picked up the green of the velvet curtains that draped the windows. Matching sofas covered in a nubbly cream-coloured material stood either side of the fireplace and looked like wonderfully inviting places to curl up after a busy day.

Michelle moved to the dining room but a glance was enough to tell her that he hadn't decorated in there because the room looked far too formal to reflect his taste. She headed to the kitchen next, smiling when she saw the rows of mugs lined up on the old Welsh dresser. Each one had a motto printed on it: *Trust me, I'm a Doctor*; *Doctor always knows best…*

'Admiring my collection?'

She jumped because she hadn't heard Dominic coming along the hall. She swung round and felt her heart give one great, bounding leap that almost catapulted it out of her chest when she saw him in the doorway. He had not only changed his trousers but his shirt as well, and he was in the process of buttoning it up. The glimpse she caught of his broad chest was more than enough to send her into a spin.

She turned to face the dresser again, trying to rid her mind of the picture of that expanse of tanned skin with its covering of crisp, dark hair. 'I...um...yes. Did you buy all these or were they bought for you?'

'The viewers send them in.'

He reached past her and she felt her breath catch when his arm brushed her shoulder as he took one of the mugs off the shelf. 'This is the latest. A lady sent it to me last week.'

Michelle took the mug from him but she was aware that her hands were shaking. '*An apple a day keeps the doctor away*,' she read dutifully, wondering if her voice sounded as dry to him as it did to her. She turned the mug round and smiled when she saw the rest of the inscription: *I'm giving up fruit!*

'It's kind of people to send them.' He took the mug from her and put it back on the shelf. 'Although I'm in danger of running out of space very soon. I'll have to get some more shelves built if they keep on arriving.'

Dominic stepped back and she let out her breath, feeling her lungs burning from the pressure. Walking to the window, he glanced at her over his shoulder. 'Did you see the view from here? It's at its best at this time of the day.'

It was an effort to make her legs walk the short distance because they felt so shaky. Michelle gripped the edge of the sink as she looked out of the window, fighting to contain the feeling that she was losing control. The view seemed to shift before her eyes, like the mirages that people reportedly saw in a desert...

'There's the swans again. Over there.'

He placed his hands on her shoulders and turned her to look at where he was pointing, and she gasped. It was so quiet in the room that he couldn't have failed to hear the betraying little sound and her heart went into overdrive.

'Michelle.'

He said her name softly and it was both a question and an answer. When she felt him turning her to face him she didn't have the strength or the will to resist. She felt his fingers tighten just a little on her shoulders, but even that fractional increase in pressure created a response inside her.

Tears sprang to her eyes when she felt the first hesitant stirrings of desire awaken inside her. This was what she had dreaded happening, and yet it didn't feel wrong to stand there with Dominic's hands holding her, to feel his breath so warm and sweet on her cheek, to feel the warmth of his body flowing into hers, even though it should have.

'Don't cry, sweetheart. I can't bear to see you unhappy.'

His voice was laced with such pain that her eyes rose to his face and she knew that she couldn't lie to him the moment she saw the anguish on his face. 'I'm scared, Dominic, because I don't know what's happening to me.'

'Don't you?' He took hold of her hand and placed it on his chest above his heart. 'Feel how my heart is racing, Michelle.'

He moved her hand away from him and placed it over her own heart. 'Feel how your heart is racing as well. Doesn't that help to explain what's going on?'

'But I don't know if it's what I want!'

'Only you can decide that, my darling. And the only way you can make such a decision is by being brave.'

The last word was swallowed up as his lips met hers in a drugging kiss that seemed to envelop her in a feeling of warmth. Michelle felt his arms go around her, felt the urgent pressure of his body as he gathered her to him, and all of a sudden everything else faded from her mind. Dominic was kissing her with such intensity and passion that there was no room for anything else.

'Michelle!'

Her name sounded raw as it exploded from his lips this time, and she shivered when she heard the desire in his voice. She tilted her face up and opened her mouth, feeling her whole body shudder when she felt the swift, sweet invasion of his tongue. It had been so long since she'd been kissed like this, with such passion, such need, that she responded helplessly.

He gasped as he broke away to shower a trail of kisses up her cheek and across her forehead. She could feel the tremors that were coursing through him and knew that he could feel how she was trembling, too. Her legs felt so weak that it was a relief when he lifted her into his arms and carried her into the living room and laid her gently down on one of the couches.

He knelt beside her and his eyes were full of warmth and passion, and something else that stirred her unbearably when she realised what it was. To have him looking at her with such tenderness was almost more than she could bear.

'Dominic, I—'

'No. Don't say anything. Not yet. Not until I've shown you what you're missing.' He kissed the corner of her mouth, the tip of her nose, the curve of her eyebrow, then looked deep into her eyes. 'I know what you're thinking, Michelle. I can hear every single argument that you're trying to muster in here.'

He laid his hand on his heart and his face twisted with agony. 'I even know that I'm being unfair to use the passion we feel for each other to convince you, but I won't apologise for it. We could have something really special but you have to want it as much as I do.'

He bent and kissed her again, not giving her the chance to say anything. Michelle held back for only a second but the passion was building again, great waves of it, making her whole body feel languid.

She twined her arms around his neck, holding him to her, letting him kiss her and kissing him back even though she knew in her heart that at some point she would have to think about what she was doing. But that would come later, when this was over—when the hungry urgings of her body had been sated.

Dominic sighed softly as he drew her full lower lip into his mouth and gently bit it. Michelle shuddered. When she felt his hand slide up the curve of her hip and follow the dip of her waist she held her breath in an agony of anticipation. The feel of his fingers caressing the underside of her breast was so wonderfully seductive that she moaned aloud. She could feel the dragging pull of desire spiralling down through her body, making it throb almost painfully, yet it was a pain of the sweetest kind.

He sank back on his heels and his eyes seemed to glow with an inner fire as he slowly unbuttoned her blouse. Michelle lay quite still, watching the play of emotions that crossed his face as he parted the two pieces of cotton. She was wearing a plain white bra beneath and she saw him smile tenderly.

'How did I know that you wouldn't be a lady who went in for lace?' he asked with such gentle amusement in his voice that she smiled back.

'I could have a whole wardrobe of sexy underwear for all you know.'

'You could indeed,' he agreed, but she could tell that his mind was no longer on the conversation as he slid his fingers under a strap and gently drew it down her arm so that the cup of the bra fell away, leaving her breast exposed to his gaze.

He stared at her for a long moment then reached out and gently—very gently—traced the tip of his finger around her nipple. 'You're beautiful, Michelle. So very beautiful…'

He bent and placed his mouth to her breast and she cried out when she felt him suckle her tender flesh. Her hands clenched at her sides because the feelings it aroused were so intense that she didn't think she could bear them.

When he did the same to her other breast she shuddered as wave after wave of sensation flowed through her. He drew her up into his arms, holding her tightly until the spasm had passed, then repeated everything he had done all over again.

She closed her eyes, letting the passion carry her away, letting it carry with it all the pain and loneliness she had endured these past years. Dominic's delight in her body healed her, made her see that maybe—just maybe—there could be more in her life than she had let herself dream about. Nothing that felt as right as this could be wrong, surely?

The first tiny doubt crept in and she stiffened. Dominic raised his head and she could feel him watching her even though she kept her eyes closed. He brushed his knuckles over her swollen mouth and she shuddered when she felt the sensations spiral through her again.

'Look at me, sweetheart,' he ordered quietly.

She opened heavy-lidded eyes and felt her heart miss a beat when she saw the understanding on his face. He knew how she felt and had recognised that fleeting moment of uncertainty almost as soon as she had. She couldn't believe that they could be so in tune but there was no denying the fact. Whilst it warmed her it also scared her because she knew that from this point on she wouldn't be able to hide her feelings from him.

'Shh. Stop that.' He kissed her quickly and his eyes were tender when he looked at her. 'I won't allow you to start torturing yourself that way. I know how much of a shock this must have been for you, Michelle, because it was a shock for me, too, when I realised what was happening.'

He lifted her hands and kissed them both in turn, his lips warm and loving as they brushed her skin. 'I'm not going to put any pressure on you. I promise you that. I don't expect you to make any rushed decision about where we go from here. This is too important to both of us to take any risks.'

'Wh-what do you intend to do, then?' she asked, and the husky sound of her own voice brought the colour to her cheeks because she'd never dreamed that she could sound so *aroused*!

'Be there if you need me. Make you happy when you're sad.' He smiled but she couldn't fail to see the fleeting expression of fear that suddenly clouded his eyes. 'Hope that you'll realise we have a future together.'

'It isn't fair...' she protested, unbearably moved by his selflessness.

'Who said that life had to be fair?' He shook his head when she went to protest again. 'No. Let's not rush this, Michelle. You need time to think about what has happened today because it has been a big step, getting this far, hasn't it?'

'Yes,' she admitted, grateful for his understanding. 'So, what happens next?'

'I take you home while I still have the will-power to let you leave,' he said with a grin, but she could hear the grate of truth in his voice that told her how much it must have cost him to let her leave.

Dominic stood up and smiled at her. 'I'll go and start the car while you get ready.'

'Fine. And, Dominic, thank you for being so understanding.'

He didn't reply, just treated her to a smile that made her heart ache. Michelle got up as soon as he left the room and quickly buttoned up her blouse. There was an old mirror over the fireplace and she went to it and straightened her hair. Her reflection was cloudy, but she couldn't fail to see the brightness in her eyes and the passion-softened curve of her mouth.

She felt a sudden fear chase through her, cold and stark after the warmth and passion she had found in Dominic's arms. Could she live with herself if she fell in love with another man? Could she find happiness in the future when she was betraying Stephen's memory?

Her thoughts shifted like ripples on a pond. It was impossible to capture them and know for certain what was right and what was wrong. She would just have to do as Dominic had said and wait to see what happened, but it wasn't going to be easy, whatever she decided.

Dominic went straight home after driving Michelle back to her flat, but he was too keyed up to sleep. He went into town and bought a paper and stocked up on a few other essentials. He made himself a large pot of coffee when he got in and took it into the living room, but just a glimpse of the sofa had him turning on his heel.

He went back to the kitchen, breathing deeply in the vain hope that it would control the extremely blatant statement his body was making. He fleetingly considered a cold shower but quickly discarded the idea. He was already suffering quite enough without inflicting any more torture on himself! Just thinking about how Michelle had looked lying on the sofa was enough to test any man's restraint, and his had been tested way beyond any reasonable limits already that day. He would drink his coffee, read his paper then get on with some work, and hope that his raging hormones would quieten down.

He spread the paper on the table and glanced at the headlines, feeling his stomach sink. The front page carried a story about Sunita Kumar, naming her as the mother of the abandoned baby. There was a photo of her sister, Meena, looking deeply upset as she hurried out of the hospital, and even a reference to his programme and the fact that it had been seeing it which had made Meena contact the hospital. For the life of him, he couldn't understand how the press had got hold of the story, but it was the kind of blatant invasion of privacy that infuriated him.

Didn't the person who had written this realise the damage he might have caused to the girl and her family?

He flicked through the rest of the news but his interest had been staled by the lead story. He thought back over everything that had happened the previous night, mentally checking that he hadn't been unwittingly to blame for the news getting out, but his conscience was clear.

He thrust the paper in the bin and went to take a shower before getting down to some of the work that was waiting for him. As he stepped under the jets of hot water he found himself wondering fleetingly if Michelle had seen the report in the paper, and what she would make of it when she did.

At least he could swear with his hand on his heart that he hadn't been in any way to blame!

CHAPTER TEN

'HEAVEN alone knows where they got the information. I've spoken to everyone who was on duty last night and they deny all knowledge of it.'

Max tossed the newspaper onto the desk. 'The Chief Executive is blazing. He's been told by the hospital trust's lawyers that the Kumar family will have a very strong case if they decide to sue for damages and can prove that the information came from a member of staff.'

'It's incredible,' Michelle said worriedly. She had arrived at work that night to find the department in an uproar over the leaked information about Sunita Kumar. She hadn't heard anything about it until then because she'd not read a paper. She had slept like a baby after Dominic had taken her home and only woken in time to get ready for work.

Her heart gave a little hiccup at the thought of Dominic and what had happened that morning before she hurriedly forced herself to concentrate. She still wasn't sure how she felt about it all and now wasn't the time to decide.

'So who did know that the girl was Meena Kumar's sister? It says here that she came to the A and E department and it was a member of our staff who dealt with her.'

'Dominic.' Max grimaced. 'According to Trisha, he was the one who spoke to Miss Kumar, and the ward nurse on Women's Surgical confirmed that Dominic had spoken to her.'

'Surely you aren't suggesting that Dominic leaked the story to the press,' she protested.

'I'm not suggesting anything,' Max said pompously. 'However, we have to face the fact that if anyone around here has the right contacts, it's Dominic Walsh.'

'But why would he do such a thing?' she exclaimed in dismay.

'I don't know,' Max said irritably. 'Maybe for publicity for his show. Every one of the papers I've seen makes some kind of a reference to *Health Matters*.'

'That's rubbish! Dominic doesn't need that kind of publicity. His show is already so popular that he wouldn't dream of stooping so low as to do a thing like that.'

'You've changed your tune, Michelle.' Max looked at her assessingly. 'A week ago you would have had the man hung, drawn and quartered for less.'

'And maybe I was wrong to think like that,' she admitted. 'I just know that Dominic isn't to blame for this.'

'Let's hope you're right,' Max said with a heavy sigh. 'Anyway, onto some good news. Lisa is improving in leaps and bounds. The police have interviewed her and Si, and they've managed to give them a description of the yob who threw that brick at the ambulance. They've put an identifit photo of him in the paper so let's hope someone will come forward with information.'

'Fingers crossed,' she agreed.

Max left shortly afterwards so she went to get started, exchanging a few commiserating words with Trisha, who was feeling guilty about what had happened over Sunita Kumar even though it hadn't been her fault. The thought that anyone from the department might have made such an unprofessional disclosure was worrying, but she refused to attribute the blame to Dominic. It simply wasn't the kind of thing he would do!

She smiled to herself as she collected the patient's notes and went to a cubicle. No wonder Max had been surprised because her attitude towards Dominic had undergone a complete reversal. She could never have believed that she would feel this way about him, and certainly couldn't have anticipated what had happened that morning. However, she didn't regret it even if she wasn't wholly ready to accept it. One step at a time seemed the best advice so she would stick to that and not look too far ahead.

A half-hour later she was ready to break the news to a patient that he had a broken ankle. Mark Smith had been learning to snowboard at the new indoor snow arena that morning and had been a little too adventurous. He had fallen and twisted his ankle badly. He'd thought that it had only been a sprain, but the continued pain had finally prompted a visit to the A and E department that night.

'A clean break, right here, Mark.' She slid the X-ray under the clips on the light-box and pointed to a hairline fracture across his fibula.

'Does that mean I'll have to have it in plaster?' he said in disgust. He was in his mid twenties, very good-looking, with dark red hair and the most soulful chocolate-brown eyes. Michelle had noticed that young Amy had been very attentive so decided to soften the blow.

'I'm afraid so. It will need support while the bones knit together, but it shouldn't take more than a month to six weeks to heal. I'll get Amy to take you to the plaster room and sort it out for you.'

'Oh, right. Great.' He brightened considerably when Amy stepped forward. 'I hope you're going to treat me gently,' he said with a wicked grin that brought the colour to the young nurse's face.

Michelle left them to it, smiling to herself as she left the cubicle. It looked very much as though her matchmaking had been spot on the mark!

'And what are you looking so pleased about, Dr Roberts?'

She spun round, unable to hide her delight when she saw Dominic. 'Hello! I wondered if you'd be in tonight.'

'I told you I would be,' he said softly, his voice throbbing in a way that made her bones feel as though they were in danger of melting.

'So you did,' she said quickly, but she knew he had sensed her reaction and that he was pleased by it. She hurried on, afraid that things were moving too fast. That wasn't what she wanted to happen if she was to stick to her decision to take everything slowly.

'I've been playing Cupid,' she informed him, lowering her voice as Amy appeared, pushing Mark in a wheelchair towards the plaster room. 'I think that patient is rather smitten by Amy so I thought I'd help smooth things along by providing them with a bit of quality time together.'

'True love blossoms over a bucket of plaster of Paris?' he teased.

'It's not the place, it's the person,' she corrected him sternly, although she found it difficult not to smile.

'Yes, ma'am! I stand corrected, although poor Mike Soames is going to have his nose pushed out of joint. I think Mike has a bit of a *thing* about Amy,' he explained when she looked quizzically at him.

'Trust me to interfere and spoil things!' she declared ruefully.

'Rubbish! You can't tell people who to love. You have to leave it up to them to make the decision.'

There was something about the way he said that which made her heart start to race. Michelle knew that he wasn't trying to press her in any way yet she felt as though she should say something.

'Dominic, I just—'

'No. You don't need to say anything.' He brushed her cheek with the back of his hand and smiled at her. 'One step at a time, Michelle.'

'That's exactly what I was thinking just now,' she admitted wonderingly.

'"Two minds with but one thought",' he quoted. 'Let's hang onto that idea and see what happens.'

She smiled at him, loving the fact that he was so sensitive to her feelings. 'Sounds good to me.'

'Good. And how does the idea of a swish night out sound to you? It's the National Television Awards dinner next week and I would really love it if you would agree to be my partner, Michelle.'

'Me? Oh, but I couldn't! I mean, there must be dozens of people you could ask...'

'But none I really want to go with. *Health Matters* has been nominated for an award and there's nothing I'd like more than to have you with me if we win.'

It was impossible to ignore the sincerity in his voice. Michelle swallowed the sudden lump in her throat. Dominic wanted her to know that she was an important part of his life now, and it meant a lot to her to realise that.

'Then, yes, I would love to go. Although I have no idea what I'm going to wear!'

He chuckled softly. 'Typically female reaction.'

'I can't help it.'

'Don't even try,' he growled. 'I love you just the way you are.'

'Do you, Dominic?'

'Yes.'

His eyes held hers and she could see that he was telling her the truth. For a moment panic overwhelmed her because she was so afraid that she would never be able to give him what he wanted. Then slowly her mind cleared and she realised with a sense of wonder that when she made her decision it could be unbiased by events of the past if that was what she wanted. She had the power to put the past behind her if she chose to do so.

'Anyhow, I'd better make a start. Maybe we can have our breaks together if it isn't too hectic?' he suggested.

'I'd like that.' She smiled at him, feeling as though a weight had suddenly been lifted. 'I really would.'

It was another busy night. Between the stabbings and beatings, the people who had overdosed on alcohol or drugs, the queue seemed never-ending.

Dominic worked through it all with a lightness in his heart that made the hours fly past. There wasn't time for he and Michelle to take their breaks together because it was far too busy. But the fleeting smiles they exchanged, the covert touches of hands were enough to keep him going. The only problem was that it soon became apparent that the rest of the team had picked up on the vibes and were highly intrigued by what was going on.

'Remember that programme that used to be on television a few years back?' Ruth Humphries said, reaching past him to snag a few more folders from the heap in the basket. 'It was called *The Love Boat*.'

'Uh-huh.' He was only half listening as he skimmed

through the case history of a young girl who had been brought in after suffering an epileptic fit.

'It's a bit like that in here tonight, between Amy making sheep's eyes at that young man with the broken ankle, and other people—whose names I won't mention—casting lustful glances at each another.'

Ruth grinned at him. 'I think they should consider doing a remake of the series and centring the action on a busy accident and emergency unit instead of a cruise ship!'

Dominic shook his head as she hurried away. He'd thought that only he and Michelle were aware of what was going on but obviously not. He experienced a momentary qualm as he wondered how he would feel if Michelle decided that she didn't reciprocate his feelings, but drove it from his mind. He couldn't afford to think like that. He had to be confident enough for both of them!

The night came to an end at last and it seemed the most natural thing in the world when he and Michelle left together. He drove her home to her flat, wishing that he could suggest another walk by the river, but he knew what would happen if he did and he refused to rush her.

She turned to him as he brought the car to a stop. 'Do you want to come in for a coffee or something?'

'The "or something" sounds tempting,' he said lightly, leaning across the seat so that he could brush her mouth with a kiss. 'Too tempting, in fact. It won't be coffee we're having if I come in, sweetheart, and it's too soon for that yet.'

'One step at a time?' she said quietly, laying her palm against his cheek.

'Yes. And it doesn't have to be a whole step either.'

He turned so that he could kiss her palm, smelling the

scent of antiseptic on her skin and marvelling at how it could be so sexy. It was an effort to concentrate on the rather convoluted sentence he had begun.

'It can be a tiptoe forward, a hop, skip and a jump or anything you want, basically.'

'You're too kind, Dominic,' she said, her eyes welling with tears.

'No tears. They're forbidden.' He brushed them away with his thumbs. 'And I'm not kind at all. If I have to wait for you, Michelle, that's what I shall do. All the best things are worth waiting for,' he added, in a deliberate attempt to lighten the mood.

She laughed softly as she reached over and kissed him. 'So they are. Right, that's me finished for the night. One more to go then back to the realms of civilisation. I'm off on Monday and Tuesday so it will give me time to catch up with my sleep.'

'And I won't be in tonight or tomorrow because we have a schedule meeting to hammer out some new ideas for the autumn. Hugh has suggested doing a couple of shows from an ER unit in Boston so we need to work out the logistics.' He sighed. 'Another week and that will be it. I'm going to miss being at St Justin's.'

'We could always offer you a permanent post,' she suggested quietly.

He frowned when he saw how still she had gone. Was his decision to opt out of hands-on medicine still an issue between them? He had hoped that she would have been convinced by now that what he did made a valuable contribution, but maybe not.

The thought suddenly made him examine how he felt about the idea of returning to medicine, and he was surprised that the concept was far more attractive than it had been. However, he knew that it would be a mistake to make a major decision about his future while his emotions were in such turmoil. He had to want to make the change for himself and not because it might improve his image in Michelle's eyes.

'I shall have to think about that,' he said lightly, trying to close his mind to the disappointment he saw in her eyes. He kissed her quickly then got out and opened the door for her and kissed her all over again, out there on the pavement with the world and his wife driving past.

He grinned as the driver of a passing van rolled down the window and shouted encouragement. 'Who said the British are an unromantic lot?'

'There's romance and there again there's *romance*,' she retorted. 'Those remarks didn't come anywhere near to my idea of what's romantic!'

'Sounds intriguing. We must explore that in more depth, but not now. You, young lady, need your sleep.'

He gave her a last lingering kiss then got back into the car. He waited until she had let herself into the house then drove away. There was a warm, fuzzy feeling inside him, as though all the sharp edges in his life had been smoothed away. Nothing seemed to irritate him, so that when another car cut in front of him he simply smiled forgiveness and waved to the driver. Love was a wonderful thing!

It was only when he drew up in front of his house that the feeling started to fade and he sighed. Love was only truly wonderful if it was reciprocated.

The rest of the weekend flew past, then Michelle used one of her days off to scour the shops for something suitable to wear at the awards dinner. She had confided in Ruth about where she was going and the other woman had insisted on accompanying her. The honour of St

Justin's was resting on Michelle looking her best, she'd declared with her tongue firmly in her cheek.

They finally found the perfect dress in a small boutique off Oxford Street. It was a French designer gown with a price tag to match its pedigree. Michelle would never have tried it on if Ruth hadn't insisted, but the moment she did so she knew it was the dress she'd been looking for.

Made from black silk with a chiffon overlay, it was so perfectly cut that it fitted her like a dream. It had tiny diamanté straps which made wearing a bra out of the question, but it looked so wonderful that she didn't have a qualm about going without. A pair of high black satin mules and matching evening bag completed the ensemble.

Michelle took a deep breath then wrote out a cheque, but their shopping trip didn't end there. Ruth whisked her to a top hairdressing salon which she had read about in one of the glossy magazines and somehow persuaded them to fit Michelle in there and then for an appointment.

'How did you manage to talk them round?' Michelle asked as they left the salon a couple of hours later. 'The receptionist told me that their appointment book is filled up months in advance.'

'Oh, a bit of name-dropping is a wonderful thing,' Ruth replied airily.

'Name-dropping? But they don't know me from Adam!' she exclaimed.

'Oh, yes, they do. A lot of people watch *Health Matters*. They've seen you on the show and when I happened to mention that Dominic was taking you to the awards dinner...well!'

Michelle shook her head in bemusement. 'I can't believe you did that.'

'The end justifies the means,' Ruth declared. She stopped and pointed to the window of a shop they were passing. 'Look at yourself and tell me that you don't look fantastic.'

Michelle looked, feeling a little glow of satisfaction spread through her when she took stock. The stylist had cut several inches off her hair and layered the sides so that it hung softly around her face. It was such a departure from her usual severe style that it was hard to believe it was really her. She looked years younger and—she had to admit it—far more attractive. Would Dominic like the change, though?

'He'll love it.'

She blinked because she hadn't realised that she'd spoken the thought out loud. 'Will he?'

'Yes. Tell me to mind my own business if you like, Michelle, but there's something going on between you two, isn't there?'

'Yes, I think so.' She saw Ruth's confusion and sighed. 'It's rather complicated…'

'And I'm poking my nose in where it isn't wanted,' Ruth said quickly. 'Sorry. Now, how about splurging on a taxi rather than taking the tube?'

Michelle nodded, wishing that she'd told Ruth the whole story because it would have been good to ask her advice. Still, it wouldn't be fair to expect someone else to tell her what to do when she had such problems making up her own mind. One step at a time, she reminded herself as a taxi drew to a stop in front of them. It might take some time to get there but Dominic had said that he was prepared to wait.

* * *

Michelle went into work on Wednesday morning to discover that Richard Hargreaves had started work the previous day. The board had rushed through his application and hired him on a trial basis for three months. Having him there helped ease some of the pressure, and the situation was further improved when the agency phoned to say that they had two experienced nurses willing to work in the department.

Dominic wasn't in that day but he phoned to say that he would collect her just after six. Michelle was glad that she was able to get away early for once as Bryan had volunteered to work the evening shift. Most of the department knew that she was going to the awards ceremony and they were expecting a full report about what happened the following day.

She hurried home and showered then started getting ready. It took her a little while until she was satisfied, but when she finally stepped in front of the mirror she couldn't help feeling pleased.

Her hair swung round her face in a glossy dark brown curtain, thanks to the wonderful new cut. Muted greeny-grey eyeshadow made her eyes look enormous, the subtle addition of liner and mascara simply adding to the overall effect. A pale base coat over her skin added a dewy sheen while the warm plum lipstick lent a hint of sophistication in keeping with the elegant dress.

She ran her hands over the silky-fine fabric, enjoying how it made the most of her slender curves. Knowing that she looked her best gave her a confidence that she'd not had before so that when Dominic rang the bell she had no qualms about going down to meet him.

He took a slow step back and stared at her. 'Wow! You look simply stunning, Michelle. Your hair, that dress...' He gulped as his gaze travelled down her legs to her feet, encased in the dainty, high-heeled mules. 'Everything!'

'So, can I take it that you won't be ashamed to be seen with me tonight?' she teased, closing the door. It was really warm that night so she hadn't bothered with a coat, not wanting to risk crushing her dress.

'I most certainly won't.' He went to kiss her then stopped. 'Am I going to ruin your lipstick?'

'Probably, but don't let that stop you.'

He kissed her softly on the mouth with the most exquisite care. 'I shall confine myself to that modest token until later.'

Michelle shivered as he offered her his hand and led her to the chauffeured limousine. Later? She hadn't got as far as wondering what might happen after the dinner, but now the idea had taken root in her head she couldn't seem to shift it. Dominic had said that he would wait, but did she want him to? Maybe it would help her make up her mind if she took the next step sooner rather than later?

The thought lingered in the back of her mind all evening long. It was such a wonderful evening, too. She had never been to such a glitzy occasion and felt nervous at first when she saw the crowds that had gathered outside the hotel to watch the celebrities arriving.

Dominic turned to her as they drew up and smiled reassuringly. 'You'll be fine, sweetheart. Just smile and keep on smiling and everyone will be more than happy.'

'OK.' She took a deep breath as the chauffeur opened the door. Dominic got out first then offered her his hand. She slid out of the seat, blinking as flashbulbs popped all around them. There was a large crowd of photographers from various newspapers and they were bombarded with questions as they made their way up the plush red carpet that had been laid across the pavement.

Dominic breathed a sigh of relief as the glass doors closed behind them. 'Now I know what a gladiator must have felt like going into the arena!'

Michelle laughed at that. 'I would have thought you'd be used to the attention by now.'

'I don't think I'll ever get used to it!' he declared pithily. He glanced round as Hugh came hurrying over and slid his arm protectively around her. 'Right, one battle fought so the next one should be easy.'

'What do you mean…?' she began.

'Michelle! Wonderful to see you. I'm so glad you decided to come.' Hugh kissed her enthusiastically on both cheeks. 'I've got an interview all lined up with the arts correspondent from *The Times*. I know you weren't expecting it, but—'

'Sorry, Hugh, but Michelle isn't giving any interviews tonight,' Dominic said firmly. 'She's here purely to enjoy herself, not do some free PR work for the show.'

'Oh, I see.' Hugh looked so downhearted that Michelle wondered if it was fair to have turned him down. However, a glance at Dominic's set face warned her not to say anything.

He led her into the bar, handing her a glass of champagne from the trays of drinks that were being offered to the guests. He seemed to know most of the people there, judging by the number who came over to speak to him, but he made a point of introducing her to everyone so that she didn't feel left out. By the time the Master of Ceremonies announced that it was time to go in for dinner, her head was reeling with names.

They were sitting right in the centre of the room and she was aware of people looking at them as they took their places. The table was occupied mainly by production crew from *Health Matters* and they made her very welcome.

Michelle smiled as she looked around. 'I was worried that I would feel a bit out of my depth, but everyone has been really lovely.'

'And so they should. A lot of people have seen the work you do because of the programme, and they realise how very special you are.' Under cover of the table, Dominic squeezed her hand. 'I'm so glad you came tonight. It means such a lot to me to have you here.'

'It means a lot to me that you asked me,' she said softly, seeing his eyes flare with an inner fire that made her pulse leap.

It was an effort to respond when Hugh sat down next to her and introduced her to his wife, Bernice. Even while she was making polite conversation with the other woman, she could feel little ripples of awareness racing through her.

She had never been so sexually aware of a man in the whole of her life. When Dominic leant forward to speak to someone across the table, she shivered. When she heard the deep rumble of his laughter, she trembled. Little by little the tension was building inside her, and the most disturbing thing of all was knowing that it was happening to Dominic as well.

The food was probably wonderful but it could have been gruel for all she tasted of it. She ate what was placed in front of her and had no idea what she had tasted a few minutes later. With so many people at the table it would have been impolite to talk solely to Dominic and yet, in a funny kind of a way, that simply seemed to heighten her awareness of him. She could speak to him if she wanted to; she could have touched him as well. The fact that she refrained from doing either simply increased her hunger.

Once the dinner was over the ceremony began. She clapped politely as each winner was announced, feeling the excitement building as the moment when they would find out if *Health Matters* had won the award for the best documentary drew closer. When the judges' decision was announced and they heard that they had won, the whole team went wild.

Michelle laughed as Hugh leapt to his feet and hugged her. Mike Soames came rushing around the table and gave her a kiss. Everyone was laughing and hugging each other and suddenly there was Dominic, bending to put his arms around her and kiss her. It seemed the most natural thing in the world to kiss him back, right there in front of everyone.

She blushed as a cheer erupted. Dominic grinned as he let her go. 'I'll have to go up to accept the award. I won't be long.'

'I'm not going anywhere,' she said softly, and knew from his sudden stillness that he had understood. She watched him walking up and her heart felt as though it was going to burst from sheer joy as it hit her how much she loved him. He was everything a woman could want, and he wanted her.

In that moment all her uncertainties melted away and she knew that she was doing the right thing. She had loved Stephen and what they'd had together had been special, but she could no longer live in the past and he wouldn't have wanted her to. It was as though she could hear his voice inside her head, giving her his blessing and telling her to live her life to the full and in that way cherish the memories they had made together. She had too much love to give to waste it.

Thunderous applause rang around the room as Dominic finished his acceptance speech. Michelle smiled at him with her heart in her eyes as he came back to the table.

'Congratulations. It's a wonderful achievement.'

'At one time I would have believed this would be the happiest day of my life,' he said softly.

'Only there are better things to come?'

'Maybe.'

She took hold of his hand, feeling the warmth and strength of his fingers as they immediately closed around hers. 'Not just maybe, Dominic. Not any longer.'

She knew that he understood what she was telling him when she felt his fingers grip hers. 'Are you sure, Michelle? I don't want you to rush and make a mistake...'

'Are you trying to talk me out of the decision I've made?' she said, treating him to a mock glare.

'No! That's the last thing I'm trying to do. I just want you to be certain.'

'I am.'

The rest of the party arrived back at the table, having each taken a turn at the microphone, so she didn't say anything else. They ordered more champagne to celebrate and Michelle accepted a glass. Dominic raised his glass and proposed a toast. 'To everyone on the team.'

'Everyone on the team,' they all repeated. Michelle raised her glass then paused when Dominic touched his glass to hers.

'To us. And to the future.'

'To us and to the future,' she echoed, and it seemed more like a promise than merely a toast.

The time seemed to drag after that. Michelle knew that Dominic was having as much trouble curbing his impatience as she was. Finally the evening came to an end and they were free to leave. Most of their party were going on to a nightclub afterwards, but Dominic shook his head when they were invited along.

'Michelle's got to work tomorrow and so have I.'

There were a lot of sympathetic groans but everyone took their refusal in the right spirit. Dominic phoned the driver to bring the car and they left. Most of the crowd had dispersed so there were only a handful of photographers waiting outside. Dominic hurried her past them with uncharacteristic brusqueness, sinking back in the seat as the car pulled away.

'I thought that would never end!' He reached for her hand and kissed her fingers, one by one. 'All I could think about was getting out of there as fast as I could.'

'Me, too,' she admitted.

'So what's it to be, Michelle? Do you want to go straight home?'

She shivered when she heard the grating note in his voice. 'Yes, please, but not to my home. Can we go back to your house instead?'

'Oh, yes,' he said softly, pulling her into his arms. 'Yes!'

CHAPTER ELEVEN

DOMINIC closed the front door as the car drove away. Michelle was standing in the centre of the hall and he could sense how nervous she was.

This must be a huge step for her, he thought tenderly. And he needed to make it as easy and as wonderful as possible.

'How about a drink?' he suggested, taking her hand and leading her into the living room.

'I'm not thirsty,' she admitted.

'Neither am I.' He framed her face between his hands, hoping that she could tell that there was nothing to be afraid of. 'I'm so glad you're here, Michelle.'

'I'm glad I came,' she whispered, reaching up on tip-toe so that she could kiss him.

Dominic groaned when he felt her mouth so soft and sweet under his. He swept her into his arms, holding her so close that he knew she couldn't fail to notice the way his body had responded immediately to the feel of hers. He kissed her deeply, letting his tongue slide between her lips in a mimicry of what he really wanted to do.

She drew back and looked at him and her face had never looked more lovely than it did right then with the moonlight streaming through the windows and bathing her in pearly light.

'Make love to me, Dominic. Please.'

'Are you sure about this, Michelle?' It was an almost superhuman effort to deny the raging of his body but he couldn't have lived with himself if he did as she'd asked and she later regretted it.

'Quite sure. It's what I want. It's...what...you... want...too.' She punctuated each word with a kiss then smiled at him. 'Isn't it?'

He didn't bother answering that question, couldn't because his self-control had snapped. He swept her into his arms again, plundering her mouth as the hunger inside him raged out of control. A tiny voice inside his head was whispering that he must take care not to frighten her but she didn't feel afraid as she returned his kiss with equal passion.

They were both trembling when the kiss ended, both deeply shaken by the speed and force of their need for each other. Dominic couldn't recall ever feeling this way before and it shook him to his soul to realise how much Michelle meant to him.

She moved out of his arms, her eyes holding his as she reached behind her and undid the zipper on her dress and let it fall in a pool around her feet. All she had on were a pair of silky black briefs and his heart seemed to go into overdrive as he stood there and looked at her.

'Your turn.'

He blinked when she spoke, raising startled eyes to her face. 'My turn?'

'Uh-huh.' She stepped towards him, letting the tips of her fingers skim down the line of tiny pearl studs that adorned the front of his starched white evening shirt. 'It's only fair that we take turns, isn't it?'

He laughed deeply, finding it incredibly erotic to be able to share a joke with her at a time like this. It was something else that had never happened to him before and it made him see how very special their relationship was.

'Far be it from me to be unfair.'

He shrugged off his jacket and tossed it onto a chair then undid his black silk bow-tie. The whispering sound of the silk as he pulled it free from his collar sounded unnaturally loud in the silence and he saw her bite her lip.

A shaft of pure red-hot passion lanced through him and he had to stop and kiss her because otherwise he might very well have passed out. He needed the taste of her like a plant needed water to survive.

The kiss lasted longer than he had planned but he didn't regret the extra seconds when he saw the glow that lit her beautiful grey eyes afterwards. It was an effort to recall what he'd been doing until she glanced pointedly at the tie he had dropped on the floor.

His hands were trembling more than a little as he set to work on the studs down the front of his shirt. They were the very devil to unfasten at the best of times and that night they defeated him. In the end he simply dragged the shirt over his head and tossed it aside then smiled wolfishly at her.

'What's next?'

'Mmm, I'll have to think about that.' She pressed a finger to her lips for a moment then slowly stepped out of her shoes. 'How about these?'

'Not bad,' he conceded because the sight of her dainty feet with their pearly-pink polished nails was sending some very strong signals to various parts of his body. He would never have believed that *toes* could be sexy, but hers were.

He took a deep breath to steady his racing heart then unbuckled his belt and drew it out of the loops. It fell to the floor with a clatter but he barely noticed because Michelle was turning her attention to the next item she intended to remove. His racing heart gave up the battle as he watched her unclip one diamanté stud from her ear-lobes and then the other. She placed them tidily on the mantelpiece then turned and smiled at him.

All of a sudden Dominic knew that he'd had enough of the game. There was only so much he could stand! He swept her into his arms, ignoring her laughing protest as he carried her to the sofa and laid her down.

'What happened to playing fair?'

'I just changed the rules,' he shot back, then kissed her and everything else he had been planning on saying disappeared from his mind. All he could think about was Michelle: how soft she felt; how warm and sweet her mouth was; how much he wanted her...

They made love right there in the living room with the moonlight streaming through the windows. Dominic knew that he would remember that moment all his life. Michelle's pleasure in his love-making moved him unbearably. It was as though she had been hungering for his touch for years. She gave herself to him with a sweet abandonment that touched his soul. He knew that he would die rather than do anything that might hurt her.

They lay for a long while after the first heady rush of passion had dimmed to a faint hunger, their limbs still entwined because they couldn't quite bear to be apart. Dominic held her in his arms until he felt her body relax into sleep and even then he couldn't bring himself to release her. Whilst she was in his arms he could keep her safe, stop anything from hurting her. She had suffered such a lot but he would make it all up to her if she would let him...

Would she?

Could she?

Or was he being a fool to hope that what had happened that night meant that she had finally put the past behind her?

As the night passed and he lay there sleeplessly, holding her to his heart, the fear seemed to grow bigger. He was so afraid that even now he might lose her!

The tantalising aroma of freshly brewed coffee woke her. Michelle opened her eyes a crack and smiled when she saw Dominic bending over her with a cup of coffee in his hands.

'What a lovely way to be woken up,' she murmured drowsily.

'Is it me or the coffee you fancy most?' he teased, smiling at her, yet she could see a faint uncertainty in his eyes that surprised her.

'You first and coffee a very poor second,' she told him, sitting up. At some point during the night Dominic had carried her into his bedroom and she looked around her curiously because she'd not really had the time or the inclination to consider her surroundings the night before.

Her heart gave a little hiccup of delight as the memory of why she had been otherwise engaged flooded into her mind. After making love to her on the sofa, Dominic had made love to her again right here in his bed and just recalling how tender he'd been was enough to make her blood heat all over again. She could never have believed that he would be such a gentle and considerate lover, but the time they had spent together had been simply magical.

'What are you thinking?' he said softly, sitting on the edge of the bed and turning her face towards him so that he could look deep into her eyes.

'That I never knew how wonderful it could be to make

love,' she admitted. 'Last night was everything I could have dreamed it would be.'

'For me, too.' He kissed her gently on the mouth then sighed as he drew back. 'I hate to be the bearer of bad news but if we have any hope of getting to work on time then we'll have to save the rest till later.'

'What time is it?' she asked immediately, and gasped when he showed her the dial on his watch. 'After seven! I'm usually there by now.'

'I know, but today is a special occasion, isn't it? It's our first morning together after all.'

Once again Michelle sensed a hint of uncertainty in his voice, which was so out of character that it alarmed her. 'Is there something wrong, Dominic?'

'It's probably me being silly. I can't believe that you're actually here and that last night...' He stopped and kissed her. 'That last night wasn't just some kind of a wonderful dream.'

'If it was a dream then I shared it with you.' She placed her hand against his cheek, wanting to reassure him because despite what he'd said she sensed that there was something worrying him. 'Maybe we can dream again tonight to see if it's just as good?'

'Maybe.' He pressed a kiss to her palm then rose to his feet and she had the horrible feeling that he was deliberately withdrawing from her.

'I'll take a shower while you drink your coffee. I'll give you a shout when the bathroom is free.'

'Fine,' she agreed, picking up the cup and making a pretence of drinking the fragrant liquid. However, the minute he disappeared she put down the cup again and wrapped her arms around her because a sudden chill seemed to have invaded her body. Dominic's uncertainty was starting to affect her, making her wonder if last night had been a mistake. Had she been a bit too hasty and rushed things? Should she have thought harder about what she was doing rather than jumping into bed with him?

After all, how well did they know each other? It wasn't as though they'd been out on dates like people normally did in the first stages of a relationship. She had a horrible feeling all of a sudden that she'd jumped in at the deep end when she should still have been dipping her toes into the water.

She took a deep breath, realising how stupid she was being. She didn't regret what had happened! It had been the right thing to do and at the right time. If Dominic had doubts then it was probably because he wasn't used to being in this kind of situation.

Michelle felt her heart overflow with tenderness at the thought. When he called that the bathroom was free she got out of bed and went to take a shower. She didn't have a change of clothes with her so she had to put on the dress again, and she laughed when she went into the kitchen and found Dominic sitting at the table, eating toast and marmalade.

'Not my usual morning attire, I'm afraid.'

'We can stop off at your flat on the way back so that you can get changed. Fancy some toast?'

'Please. I'm quite hungry this morning although normally I don't eat breakfast.' She grinned at him and earned herself a rueful smile in return.

'I wonder what you were doing to work up an appetite,' he said drily, getting up to pop a couple more slices of bread into the toaster.

'That would be telling.' She reached across the table when he sat down again, letting her hand rest lightly on his as she looked deep into his eyes. 'You would tell me if there was something worrying you?'

'Yes.' He squeezed her hand and his tone was pensive all of a sudden. 'I suppose I'm just afraid that we might have rushed things.'

'We'? It had never entered her head he might feel like that and it momentarily threw her off balance. Did Dominic regret what had happened?

It was an effort to pretend that nothing was wrong when he looked at her. 'Do you think we have, Michelle?'

'I'm not sure,' she said softly, hoping that he couldn't hear the pain in her voice. If Dominic had regrets, surely that was an indication that his feelings for her weren't nearly as deep as she'd thought them to be? She had believed in her innocence that he was in love with her but she could have made a mistake about that.

The bread suddenly popped up out of the toaster and he got up with an alacrity that made her feel slightly sick. It was blatantly obvious that he was finding the situation difficult to handle and it simply made her feel worse.

They finished their breakfast in record time then Dominic collected his car keys and jacket. He paused by the front door and his expression was so grave that her heart seemed to come to a dead stop.

'I think we need to talk about what has happened, Michelle. Will you come back here tonight and we can discuss it over dinner?'

She nodded quickly, not wanting to say too much in case he guessed how scared she was. 'Of course. We'd better get to work.'

'Of course.' He opened the door and stepped back so that she could precede him from the house. She had just set her foot on the top step when there was a bright flash and she looked up to see a camera being pointed at them.

Dominic swore succinctly as a dozen more flashes followed in rapid succession. 'Blasted press! Let's get out of here.'

He hurried her down the steps to his car, ignoring the questions that were hurled at them from the waiting reporters. Michelle slid into the seat and attempted to fasten her seat belt, but her hands were shaking so much that she had trouble sliding the buckle into its clasp.

Dominic reached over and snapped it shut then squeezed her hands. 'I'm sorry. I didn't realise that they were camped outside otherwise I would have used the back door.'

'It doesn't matter,' she said hollowly, but she knew that it did. The thought of having her photograph splashed across the tabloids for the whole world to see made her feel sick. She was still wearing the same dress that she'd worn to the awards dinner so it didn't take much intelligence to work out that she must have spent the night with Dominic at his house. It felt as though what they had done had been cheapened because of it.

They drove back into London in silence. Michelle couldn't have put her feelings into words if she'd wanted to, and maybe Dominic was equally upset. It was probably one thing to sleep with her but quite another to let the general public know what had gone on!

She hurried up to her flat and changed into a skirt and blouse, dragging her hair back into its customary bun. Seeing it hanging silkily around her face was too poignant a reminder of the previous night and she couldn't deal with it right then.

They were late arriving for work but nobody remarked on it because they were far too interested in hearing about what had happened at the dinner. Michelle did her best but it was hard to keep on repeating the story over and over when her mind kept whizzing back to what had happened after the ceremony had ended. She had slept with Dominic because she loved him, but had she been a fool to imagine that he felt the same?

It was a relief when they had a full-blown emergency case brought in and she was forced to stop thinking about it while she dealt with a young girl who had been found unconscious in the street, having taken an over-dose of heroin. But deep down she knew that it was only a temporary reprieve. At some point soon she would have to find out the answer.

Dominic knew that he hadn't handled things well. He should have realised that there was a strong possibility the press would have followed them home. Michelle had looked so upset when they'd got into the car that it had torn his heart to shreds.

Was she ashamed of what they had done?

He gritted his teeth and got on with the job, but every reference to the dinner was an added torment. He loved her so much but how could he fool himself into believing that she felt the same? Maybe she had wanted him last night, but it might have been no more than a phys-ical hunger. She was a normal red-blooded woman with all the usual desires, desires that she had buried for a long time. He had been ready and *willing* to satisfy them, but it wasn't proof that she loved him. Hell!

He was so screwed up from thinking about it that he knew he had to get away before he made a mistake. Fortunately, the department was fairly quiet, apart from the young heroin addict who had been rushed in, and Michelle was dealing with her.

He told Ruth that he was taking a break, but instead of going to the canteen, he went to the women's surgical ward to see Sunita Kumar. Her sister, Meena, was with her, as well as an older couple whom he took to be their parents.

He didn't stay long because he was very much aware that he might be intruding. He also sensed a certain hostility, which surprised him until he bumped into Max, who explained in his usual pompous fashion that he hoped Dominic wasn't responsible for the story about Sunita that had appeared in the papers.

He was so staggered by the suggestion that all he could do was deny it. However, it left a nasty taste in his mouth, especially when he found himself wondering if Michelle believed that he'd had a hand in the affair. He resolved to make sure that she understood it had had nothing to do with him when they talked that night then sighed as he made his way back to the department.

The list of things they needed to discuss was growing by the hour!

'That's fine, Christopher. Just lie still now. You've been a really brave little boy.'

Dominic smiled at the eight-year-old boy. The Rosen family had only just moved to the area and were having problems finding a GP who would add them to his list, which was why Mrs Rosen had brought her son to the hospital. The child had been complaining of soreness and swelling in his joints, as well as pains in his abdomen. There was also a raised, purplish rash on his buttocks and the backs of his legs and arms. Dominic had mentally run through a list of possibilities and still hadn't completely made up his mind what was wrong with the child.

'Will he be all right? When I saw the rash I immediately thought that it could be meningitis.' Mrs Rosen
looked worried to death as she stroked her son's face.
'He isn't having any problems with light, though, and
his neck isn't stiff.'

'It's good to hear a parent who's so aware of what to
look out for,' Dominic said sincerely. 'Meningitis was
the first thing I thought of as well. Not every case pres-
ents with the full range of symptoms. A child can have
meningitis and not have a stiff neck or photophobia—
an aversion to light. That's why it is so hard to diag-
nose.'

'Do you think that's what Christopher has, then?' the
woman exclaimed in dismay.

'No. The rash isn't right. A meningitis rash isn't raised
like this one. It also doesn't disappear when you place
a glass over the spots and press it lightly. I'm going to
order some blood tests to be done and ask one of the
other doctors for an opinion, but I have a feeling that it
might be Henoch-Schönlein purpura.'

'I've never even heard of that!' Mrs Rosen said worriedly.

'It's not as bad as the name suggests,' he reassured
her. 'It's caused by inflammation of the small blood ves-
sels, which causes them to leak into the skin, joints, kid-
neys and intestine. It sometimes occurs after a child has
had a sore throat, although it can be the result of some
kind of allergic reaction to a drug or certain food.'

'Christopher had a terribly sore throat a few days before we moved. I didn't have time to take him to the
doctor and it seemed to clear up on its own. Are you
saying it could be that which has caused him to be ill
now?'

'I can't say for sure, but it's a possibility.' He smiled

at the woman when he saw how distressed she looked. 'Don't start blaming yourself, Mrs Rosen. These things happen. Anyway, let's get the blood tests done then we'll know for certain. And I'll ask Dr Roberts if she will come and take a look at Christopher as well.'

He left Ruth to take the blood and went to find Michelle. She was just leaving Resus and he frowned when he saw her dejected expression.

'Something wrong?' he asked, going to meet her.

'A patient just died. Heroin overdose,' she explained a little flatly.

She seemed ill-at-ease and tense, which immediately made him start to feel the same. He couldn't shake off the feeling that it was more than the death of her patient that was troubling her, difficult though that must have been.

It was impossible to cross-question her there in the middle of A and E so he had to be content with a commiserating smile. 'Tough luck. Maybe this isn't a good moment but I wondered if you would take a look at a young boy for me. I think it might be Henoch-Schönlein purpura, but I want to be certain that I'm not missing something vital.'

'Of course,' she said quickly. She followed him back to the cubicle and Dominic swiftly introduced her to Mrs Rosen and Christopher.

He stood to one side, watching as she made a thorough examination of the child. She spoke to him the whole time, reassuring him, and Dominic smiled wistfully. She would make a wonderful mother because she was so natural with children.

Dominic took a deep breath as his mind suddenly sped off, carrying that thought to its logical conclusion—or logical to him. He could just imagine how it would feel to see her beautiful body swollen with his baby, to know that their love had created a new life. Children were something he had thought about only in passing; he hadn't sat down and decided that he wanted them. But all of a sudden he knew that he ached to be a father so long as Michelle would be the child's mother...

'I'm ninety per cent certain that you're right.'

He jumped when she spoke to him. He pasted a sickly smile to his mouth when he saw the puzzled expression in her eyes. It was obvious that she had noticed his reaction and was wondering what had caused it.

What indeed! he thought before he quickly confined his thoughts to Christopher Rosen. Michelle agreed that they should admit the little boy for observation until they had the results of the tests then went on her way while he made the arrangements. It all took some time because there was a problem finding the child a bed.

In the end everything was sorted out and Mrs Rosen thanked him before she hurried after the porters as they wheeled her son to the lift. Dominic was just about to go and see the next patient when Trisha told him that Hugh had phoned while he'd been busy and had asked him to get in touch as soon as he could.

He sighed as he went to the office and put through a call, wondering what the latest panic was. He felt his heart sink when Hugh informed him that they'd had to bring forward the date of their trip to Boston because the consultant in charge of the ER unit had realised he would be away when their meeting had been originally scheduled. Hugh had booked them both on a flight that very night and nothing that Dominic could say would persuade him that he couldn't go. It would be a tight squeeze to fit in the filming as it was and a lot of money had already been invested in the project, as Hugh was quick to point out.

He hung up, feeling as though he didn't know if he was on his head or his heels. He had desperately wanted to talk to Michelle that night and clear up any misunderstandings that might have arisen, but instead he would be flying across the Atlantic. He wouldn't even get a chance to say much to her that afternoon because he would have to go home and pack. Talk about bad timing!

His heart sank. Surely she wouldn't believe that he'd done it deliberately to avoid having to talk to her?

Michelle dealt with a half a dozen minor injuries then decided that she would take her lunch-break. Max was showing the two new agency nurses around the department so he could hold the fort, and John was due in at one. She was just stepping into the lift when Dominic called her and she put out her hand to stop the doors closing.

'Are you coming for lunch?'

'I don't have the time,' he explained, stepping smartly into the lift. He pressed the button for her floor then sighed. 'Hugh has booked us both on a flight to Boston to finalise arrangements for the US version of the show. I think I mentioned that we're doing a series from an ER unit there to show the differences between emergency care in the States and England.'

'You're going today?' she exclaimed in dismay.

'I know how you feel, sweetheart. It was a blow for me, too.' His eyes were shadowed. 'We need to talk, Michelle—that's obvious, isn't it? But we're not going to have the chance until I get back.'

'There's not much you can do about it,' she said carefully, wondering why she felt so let down. It wasn't as if Dominic had *deliberately* chosen to fly over to America at this exact moment. Was it?

The thought made the blood pound in her ears and she swallowed hard as panic set in. Dominic must have sensed how she was feeling because he pulled her into his arms.

'I'm sorry, Michelle. I never intended this to happen—any of it. Believe me when I say that I never wanted to hurt you.'

She had no idea what he meant and there was no time to ask as the lift arrived at her floor. Dominic let her go as the doors opened.

'I'll try to phone you, but it gets a bit hectic when we're on a research trip. I'll be back at the end of next week and we can talk then.'

'Fine,' she agreed dully.

He blew her a kiss as the lift doors closed, ready to carry him back down to the ground floor. Michelle went to the canteen then changed her mind, realising that she was too tense to eat.

Everything would be fine, she told herself as she went and sat in the residents' lounge. As soon as Dominic came back they would talk and get everything straight. She just had to hold onto the thought that it would work out if she wanted it to, and she did. She did!

Somehow she managed to convince herself and got through the rest of the day. Dulcie greeted her plaintively, obviously put out by the fact that she'd been left on her own for a whole night. Michelle spent the evening making a fuss of her and went to bed early, trying not to think about the previous night and how the hours had flown past as she'd lain in Dominic's arms.

She went into work the following day but it soon became apparent that there was something wrong. People kept looking at her really oddly, and several times she saw Ruth smiling commiseratingly at her. In the end she plucked up her courage and asked Ruth what was going on because she couldn't stand it any longer.

'You mean you haven't seen the papers?' Ruth said worriedly.

When Michelle shook her head she took her into the staffroom and closed the door. There was a pile of papers on the table and Ruth picked one up and handed it to her without saying a word.

Michelle's heart sank when she saw the picture of herself and Dominic leaving his house the previous day splashed across the front page. However, it was the headline that made her start to shake uncontrollably.

'Wh-where did they get this story from?' she asked, her mouth so dry that she could barely get out the words.

'I don't know.' Ruth looked upset. 'Nobody here knew that you'd been married, Michelle, let alone that your husband had died so tragically.'

'No.' She took a deep breath but the pain was too deep to go away. The headline glared back at her: TRAGIC DOCTOR FINDS HAPPINESS AT LAST. The story went on to tell in detail how Stephen had died ten years ago of a brain tumour. Much was made of the fact that she and Dominic had met when he had filmed his show at the hospital.

There was a lot more—far too much to take in, not that it really mattered. There was only one person who could have leaked the story to the press, just one person who had known about Stephen, and that was Dominic.

He had used her to gain publicity for his programme. It was as simple and as painful as that.

CHAPTER TWELVE

HUGH hadn't been pleased when Dominic had cut short their visit to the States. Although they had agreed in principle that the programme could go ahead, there were still a lot of details that needed finalising. However, Dominic had been unable to curb his impatience to get home any longer. He had phoned Michelle at least a dozen times, both at work and at home, and on each occasion he had failed to speak to her. It was obvious that there was something seriously wrong and he needed to sort it out—fast!

He took a taxi from Heathrow straight to St Justin's but she wasn't there. Trisha informed him rather curtly that she had taken a few days off, although she didn't go into detail. He had the distinct impression that he was *persona non grata*, in fact, and his anxiety simply increased tenfold. What the hell was going on?

Another taxi took him to Michelle's flat. He paid the driver and ran up the steps to the front door and pressed the bell. He was so afraid that she wouldn't be there that he felt quite sick, but a moment later she answered.

'It's me,' he said curtly. 'I need to speak to you.'

She didn't say anything, simply unlocked the door and let him in. He hurried up the stairs, hesitating when he saw that her door was ajar even though she hadn't come out to meet him. If he'd needed proof that something was wrong, he had it in spades.

She was standing in the middle of the living room when he went in. She looked pale and gaunt, the sombre black sweater and skirt she was wearing more suited to a funeral than a day of leisure. Her hair was dragged back from her face, emphasising the total lack of colour in her cheeks and the inky shadows under her eyes, and his fearful heart grew even more afraid.

'What's going on, Michelle?' he asked quietly, because he could barely speak.

'I happen to have a deep dislike of people trying to use me,' she said flatly.

'Use you? I'm sorry, but I don't know what you're talking about.' He ran his hand through his hair, feeling suddenly out of his depth. He was being cast in the role of villain but he had no idea what he was guilty of.

'At least pay me the courtesy of not lying!' she shot back, and he could see the anger that had lit her eyes. She picked up a newspaper from the coffee-table and thrust it towards him. 'I hope you're satisfied. Did you get enough publicity or are you hoping for more?'

He stared at the picture of them leaving his house and shook his head. 'I didn't arrange for the photographers to be there that morning, Michelle, if that's what you think.'

'It's not the photo that bothers me, it's the story. You really should check it out to see if they got everything straight, the way you told it to them. It would be a shame to be misquoted after you went to so much trouble.'

He skimmed through the report with a growing sense of horror. 'Where on earth did they get all this from?' he began, before his mind suddenly added up what he'd read and what she'd said.

'You think I gave the journalist this story,' he said flatly, wondering how it was possible to keep functioning when it felt as though the bottom had suddenly dropped out of his world. He couldn't believe that she would think he had done such a thing yet he only had to look at her set face to know it was true.

'Nobody else knew about Stephen. Nobody else knew how he had died or that I'd been married. You are the only person I have ever told, Dominic, so it seems quite logical to me that you are the only one who could have given the reporters that information.'

She stared at him and he saw the pain that crossed her face. 'Why did you do it? Was it for the publicity? I wonder how many more viewers it will have attracted to your show?'

He didn't know what to say, didn't know if he wanted to say anything, in fact. She believed that he would have deliberately set out to hurt her for the sake of a television programme?

Suddenly he knew that he couldn't stay there because it was too painful. He swung round on his heel and made for the door. He heard her footsteps behind him, felt her hand touch his arm, but he shook her off.

'Tell me that it wasn't you, Dominic.'

Her voice shook and for a moment he almost relented, but he knew deep down that it wouldn't work. If it was to mean anything then Michelle had to know in her own heart that he would never ever have used her like that. If he tried to convince her, he would always be wondering if she really believed it or had simply allowed herself to be persuaded, like he had *persuaded* her that they had a future together. Deep in her heart, who did she really love? Him or Stephen, the man she had married?

He felt tears well to his eyes as he opened the front door. Somehow he found his way down the stairs and, even more amazingly, managed to flag down a taxi. He asked the driver to take him home to Richmond then sat in the back, too numb with pain to think. It felt as though his whole life had fallen apart and he didn't know how to put it back together again. Michelle didn't love him. How could he stand it?

The days dragged. Michelle busied herself with work, hoping it would help to ease the pain, but it just seemed to get worse. Dominic had phoned Max to say that he wouldn't be coming to St Justin's any more. He'd made the excuse that they had enough film to complete the programmes they'd planned, but she knew it was because he didn't want to see her. There were a number of approaches from various newspapers interested in her story, but she refused to speak to them and eventually the interest died down.

The rest of the staff were so careful about what they said when she was around that sometimes she wanted to scream, but she knew it was because they cared about her and that she should be grateful. She simply set her mind to getting her life back on track—back on the old track rather than the new one she had daydreamed about so briefly—and gradually everyone started behaving normally.

The one bit of good news was that Sunita Kumar's parents had decided to stand by their daughter. Sunita and her baby son left the hospital with little fuss and returned to Leicester. When it was discovered that a reporter following up on Lisa's accident had found out about Sunita when he'd made an unauthorised visit to Women's Surgical, Michelle felt deeply relieved. She would have hated to think that Dominic had been to blame for that leak as well.

Two weeks after Dominic had walked out of her flat they received an alert from Ambulance Control to tell them they were being put on standby. An aircraft flying out of Heathrow had experienced problems with its undercarriage on take-off and it had been decided that it was too dangerous to let it continue. It had been advised to return to the airport and was presently circling while it burnt off its fuel. Max called everyone together and ran through the plans that had been drawn up for just such an emergency.

'We shall be one of six teams who will respond to the emergency. Because we are the closest to the airport, the most severely injured casualties—if there are any—will be ferried straight here and the rest dispersed throughout Greater London.'

He turned to Richard Hargreaves. 'You'll be assisted by surgeons from Orthopaedics and there will be a full complement of staff on standby in Theatre.'

'Who's going to the airport?' Michelle asked.

'You, me, Sandra and Ruth,' Max said promptly. 'It's just as we planned so everyone should know what to do.'

Michelle followed the others from the room, praying that all the preparations would be unnecessary and that the plane would land safely. Richard Hargreaves went with her and he sighed when they were outside.

'Sounds like a big one this time,' he observed.

'Let's hope they land all right,' she said, her mind running through the list of what she needed to take with her.

'Look, Michelle, I've been meaning to have a word with you. It just never seems to be the right moment.'

She looked at him in surprise. 'And you think this is the right time?'

'No.' He looked sheepish. 'But if I don't say it now

then I never will. It was me who gave that story about you to the papers.'

'You? But I don't understand. How could you have told them anything when I don't even know you?'

'Remember me saying that I thought we'd met before when Max introduced us?' He hurried on when she nodded. 'We had. I just couldn't remember where at first. I was a houseman on the ward where your husband was treated. I remembered his case because it was so tragic. It just took me a while to make the connection.'

'I see. But why did you tell the reporter?' she said in confusion.

'I didn't mean to! It was purely an accident.' He sighed. 'I went for a drink with an old friend from university the night of the awards dinner. He happened to mention something about it and I told him about you going with Dominic and all of sudden I realised where I'd met you before. I never gave it a second thought when I told him about your husband, but I realised later that I should have. He's a journalist, you see.'

'So it was him who wrote the story about me?' She sighed when Richard nodded. 'I wish you'd told me this before.'

'I didn't have any idea that it was all down to me until a couple of days ago. We met up again and he thanked me for the tip-off.'

Richard sounded disgusted. 'I told him in no uncertain terms that he wouldn't be getting any more tips like that, but that doesn't make up for what I did. I'll understand if you tell Max and he decides not to keep me on.'

'It would be silly to do that,' she said quietly, struggling to absorb what she'd learned. She felt a rush of relief hit her. Dominic hadn't been to blame in any way. It had all been a horrible mistake!

'Thanks, Michelle. I really appreciate that.'

Richard looked relieved as he hurried off to get ready. Michelle followed his example and went to fetch the protective jacket and trousers that she would need to wear. Everyone was waiting in the foyer and she joined them just as the first of the ambulances arrived.

Ruth looked at her curiously when she sat next to her on the bench seat. 'You're looking a bit brighter. Did Richard say something to cheer you up?'

'Yes.' She took a deep breath, knowing that she could trust Ruth not to say anything to the others just yet. 'He told me that it was him who leaked that story to the press. Oh, it wasn't done deliberately, but you realise what it means?'

'That Dominic wasn't to blame.' Ruth gave her a hug. 'So what are you going to do about it?'

'Apologise to him, of course.'

'Attagirl!'

Ruth didn't say anything else. Michelle sank back on the seat as they sped to the airport, but her stomach was churning with nerves. Would Dominic accept her apology, though? And would it make any difference? Suddenly she wished that she had a crystal ball and could see the answers!

The airport was buzzing by the time they arrived. They went to the operations room to be briefed then made their way through the terminal. They would be stationed on the apron well away from the runway until they were given the all-clear. Fire was the biggest risk when a plane made an emergency landing, and the airport's own fire crews were standing by in readiness.

Michelle was following the others when she heard someone calling her. She looked round and gasped when she saw Hugh's wife, Bernice. 'What are you doing here?'

'Hugh and Dominic are on that plane!' Bernice was almost beside herself. 'They were on their way to Boston for another meeting.'

'On the plane?' she repeated, feeling the blood drain from her head.

'Yes! Oh, I can't stand it!' Bernice started to sob but Michelle was unable to think of anything to say to comfort her. The thought that Dominic was in such danger was more than she could bear.

Her legs were trembling so hard that it was a wonder she could walk, but she made herself follow the others. There was a knot of emergency personnel gathered on the tarmac and nobody took any notice of her. She looked round for the St Justin's staff and spotted them at the far side of the group.

She started towards them then stopped when she thought she heard someone calling her name. There were so many people about that it was hard to pick out one familiar face from the crowd. The knot of people suddenly shifted and all of a sudden there was Dominic hurrying towards her...only it couldn't be him because he was in that plane that was about to make an emergency landing...

A hand gripped her arm, holding her upright as the ground began to rock beneath her feet. Michelle closed her eyes and took several deep breaths then opened them and found herself staring into a wonderfully familiar pair of green ones.

'I thought you were on the plane...'

'We got stuck in traffic...'

They both spoke together and both stopped. She saw him take a deep breath. 'I've missed you like hell,

Michelle. If there's a chance that we can straighten out this mess then—'

'There's nothing to straighten out, or at least not so far as that newspaper article is concerned,' she said quickly. 'Richard Hargreaves told me that he had inadvertently leaked the story to the press.'

'Oh, I see.' He shrugged. 'Well, so long as you know that I'm not the culprit, that's all that matters.'

'It isn't. What matters is the fact that I imagined you would do such a rotten thing.' She felt her eyes sting with tears. 'I don't know how to apologise to you, Dominic.'

'No? I can think of a way,' he said in a tone that made her heart start to race.

'Can you? And will that help to sort out all the other problems we seem to have?'

'Probably not, because we need to talk, Michelle. But it will go a long way towards helping us work out what we want to do.'

'That's easy,' she said softly. 'I want you, if you'll have me after the mess I've made of everything.'

He closed his eyes and she heard him groan. 'Fancy finding out that your dearest wish has just come true at a moment like this. You have impeccable timing, Michelle Roberts.'

'Maybe we could work on improving it. Perhaps you could give me a few tips.'

'Maybe I can,' he growled, then looked round as a buzz of expectation ran through the group. 'Looks like the plane is coming in to land. I'd better leave you to get on with it.'

'Will I see you later?' she asked quickly.

'You can depend on it.'

He touched her lightly on the cheek then moved out

of the way as they were told to board the ambulances. Michelle took her place, feeling the tension mounting as the driver tuned the radio to the tower frequency so that they could listen to the captain as he made his approach.

Everyone was holding their breath as the plane came in to land, but it was a perfect touchdown. Most of the emergency crews were told to return to base whilst the staff from St Justin's went to check that nobody needed any medical attention.

There were a few who were distressed by what had happened but nobody had been injured so they were soon free to leave. Michelle went back to St Justin's and counted the seconds until it was time for her to go home.

She stepped out of the doors and right into Dominic's arms, and knew that was the place she wanted to be for the rest of her life!

Dominic raised his head when he became aware of a strange noise. He groaned when he realised that most of St Justin's A and E department were gathered on the forecourt, cheering. He gave Michelle a quick kiss then took hold of her hand.

'How about finding someplace a little more private?'

'You have the most wonderful ideas, Dr Walsh,' she murmured.

'Oh, I have even better ones when I get going,' he assured her, feeling the shiver that rippled through her. If they hadn't had an audience he would have kissed her again, but he managed to contain himself until they were in the relative privacy of his car.

'I love you, Michelle,' he said softly, holding her close. 'I want you to hold onto that thought while we talk because it's the only thing that really matters.'

'I love you, too.' She kissed him gently on the lips then sat back in the seat.

They drove straight to his house because Dominic knew it was what they both wanted. He let them in and kissed her again, then once more before he was able to drag himself away and lead her into the living room. Michelle sat on the sofa and smiled at him.

'It feels like home when I come here. Does that sound very presumptuous?'

'No.' He kissed her again, butterfly-light kisses which he scattered at random across her face. 'It sounds marvellous, to be honest, because I never thought I'd hear you say such a thing.'

He cupped her face in his hands, seeing the love that lit her eyes, feeling it warming away the cold spots that had settled in his heart during the last few weeks. 'I never thought you would get over Stephen,' he said simply.

'Neither did I. But Stephen and what I felt for him are in the past. It's you I love now, Dominic. You I want to spend the rest of my life with. I just needed you to make me see how wrong it was to waste it by looking back instead of forward.'

'You can't imagine how it feels to hear you say that.' He rested his forehead against hers, knowing that she could feel him trembling.

'If it feels anywhere near as good to you as it does to me, then I do understand.' She bit her lip and he looked at her sternly.

'What? You aren't allowed to have secrets—it's a house rule.'

She laughed. 'Is it indeed? I was just thinking how close we came to losing all this. Would you have agreed to see me if I'd phoned you up?'

'Is that what you'd decided to do?' He felt his heart swell with joy when she nodded.

'Yes. As soon as Richard told me this morning that he was the source of that newspaper story, I knew I had to apologise. I feel so wretched about blaming you, Dominic. Can you forgive me?'

'Yes, although at one point I didn't think that I could.' He kissed the tip of her nose, thinking about the painful battle he had fought with himself in the last few weeks. He had desperately wanted to go to her and try to clear up the misunderstanding, but he'd refused to swallow his pride.

'I told myself that you couldn't possibly care for me if you didn't know, without me having to tell you, that I would never hurt you.'

'I *should* have known but I was afraid. I thought maybe you'd realised that you'd made a mistake, got in too deep and wanted to put an end to our relationship. I told myself all sorts of crazy things, Dominic, because I was scared.'

'What of?' he asked, puzzled.

'Of making a mistake, of being hurt, of…of all kinds of things! When you've lived such a quiet life as I've led for the past ten years there's a lot to be afraid of.'

'I love you, Michelle. I love you with all my heart. Does it help if I tell you that?'

'Oh, yes,' she whispered. 'It makes all the difference. I love you, too, Dominic.'

'Sounds like we're making real progress here,' he murmured, letting his lips find hers again. The kiss was long and satisfying and it would have lasted even longer if the phone hadn't rung.

Dominic sighed as he dragged himself away so that he could pick up the receiver. It was Hugh, wanting him

to reschedule their missed flight. He cut him off mid-
sentence.

'I'm rather busy at the moment, Hugh. I'll phone you
back... No, don't come round. I'll phone you tomorrow
or the day after.'

Hugh was still protesting when Dominic gently put
the receiver back on its rest. He got up and pulled the
plug from its socket.

Michelle laughed. 'You can't do that!'

'I just have,' he said. He held out his hands and drew
her to her feet. 'I don't intend for there to be any inter-
ruptions for the rest of the evening.'

'Only the evening?' She raised a delicate brow.

'And the night, and the morning and the afternoon
and—'

'I get the message!' She laughed. 'Although we might
just have to find enough time to go and fetch Dulcie.
She won't be pleased if she's left on her own too long.'

'She's never *pleased*,' he retorted, drawing her into
his arms and kissing her. He sighed as he ran a gentle
hand down her spine and felt her tremble. 'Does this
mean that I have to adopt that feline bundle of terror?'

'She can be really sweet when you get to know her.'

'It must be love,' he said darkly, lifting her into his
arms to carry her into the bedroom. 'Because I'm even
prepared to believe you.'

'So long as you believe that I love you?'

'I do.' He set her gently down on the bed then sat
beside her. 'And if you hadn't loved me now, I would
have found a way to make you in the future.'

'Once you swallowed your pride?' she teased.

'I didn't say I was perfect, did I?'

'No, and neither am I. Thank you for waiting for me,
Dominic. Thank you for caring.'

'All the best things are—'

'Worth waiting for,' she finished for him, then drew him down into her arms. 'But sometimes it's nice not to have to wait *too* long.'

EPILOGUE

THREE months later...

'I'm going to be late!'

'Oh, no, you're not.' Dominic grinned as he pulled Michelle down into his arms and kissed her. He brushed the tip of her nose with his, wondering how it was possible to be so happy. Each day just seemed to get better, in fact.

'I put the alarm clock forward an hour. It's only six a.m., not seven,' he explained smugly.

'I would ask you why you did it, only I think I can guess!'

She kissed him, her eyes so full of love that he thought his heart was going to explode. Snuggling down into his arms, she sighed in contentment. 'Have any more good ideas, like how we're going to make the best use of this extra hour?'

'Oh, I'm full of ideas, some better than others.' He felt her mouth curl as she smiled, and ran his hand down the gentle curves of her body. 'I'll show you a couple in a few minutes but there's something I wanted to ask you first and something I wanted to tell you as well.'

'Sounds intriguing,' she murmured lazily.

'Uh-huh.' He kissed her again, holding her close so that he could feel the warmth of her body just for the sheer joy of it. 'How do you fancy getting married next week?'

'What? Did you just say what I thought you did?' She sat up and stared at him.

'I did.' Dominic took a deep breath but it was difficult to keep his mind on what he'd been saying with her sitting there like that, her beautiful body naked to his gaze.

She must have guessed what was going through his mind because she sank back down and covered herself with the sheet. 'That comes later. I want an explanation first.'

'You hard-hearted woman, letting a poor man suffer like this…'

'You really will suffer if you don't explain yourself!'

He laughed when he heard the loving threat in her voice. 'All right, then. I had this brilliant idea that we should get married abroad to save the press hounding us. I've booked everything, and if you agree we can be married next week in Barbados. How does that sound to you?'

'Absolutely perfect,' she said softly, kissing him on the cheek. 'I hated the idea of our wedding turning into a media circus but now we can slip away and nobody will know a thing about it until it's a *fait accompli*.'

'Good. That's what I was hoping you'd say.' Dominic returned her kiss then dragged himself away with obvious reluctance, wondering how the next thing he had to tell her would be received. He had thought long and hard about the decision, but he knew he was doing the right thing.

'I've decided to take a back seat for a while and let someone else present *Health Matters*. Max has offered me a part-time registrar's post at St Justin's and—'

'No!' Michelle sat up again and he blinked when he saw the annoyance on her face.

'You mean you don't want me working there?' he said uncertainly.

'No, I mean that I don't want you to give up what you're doing.' She looked him straight in the eye. 'What you do makes a difference, Dominic. I know that now. I don't want you giving it up because you believe it's what I want you to do.'

'It's not just that,' he began.

'Isn't it? Can you put your hand on your heart and swear that what I said to you in the beginning hasn't influenced you?'

He sighed. 'No, I suppose not, but I really do want to take this job.'

'Then maybe you can find a way to combine both jobs. Anything is possible if you want it enough,' she said firmly.

'Are you sure you'd be happy with that?' he asked, loving her more than ever at that moment. She wanted only what was best for him. That he wanted the same for her just made it even more perfect.

'I'll be happy whatever you choose to do. It's you I love, Dominic—the person you are, not the job that you do.' She took a deep breath and he saw the oddest expression cross her face before she seemed to come to a sudden decision.

'And our baby won't care if he has a television star or a doctor for his father.'

'Our baby?' he repeated numbly. He stared at her. 'Are you saying that you...that we...that...?'

'Yes. You are going to be a father, Dominic Walsh, in...oh, a little over six months' time. How do you feel about the idea?'

'How do I feel? Wonderful!'

He swept Michelle into his arms and kissed her, hearing her delighted laughter. Drawing back, he looked deep into her eyes.

'I love you, Michelle. For always and ever.'

'I love you, too. For always and for ever.'

They kissed again and it was like the seal being put on their future.

Forrester Square

LEGACIES . LIES . LOVE .

*The Kinards, the Richardses and the Webbers were
Seattle's Kennedys, living in elegant Forrester Square—
until one fateful night tore these families apart.*

*Now, twenty years later, memories and secrets are about
to be revealed...unless one person has their way!*

Coming in October 2003...

THE LAST THING SHE NEEDED
by Top Harlequin Temptation® author
Kate Hoffmann

When Dani O'Malley's childhood friend died, she suddenly found
herself guardian to three scared, unruly kids—and terribly
overwhelmed! If it weren't for Brad Cullen, she'd be lost. The sexy
cowboy had a way with the kids...and with her!

Forrester Square...Legacies. Lies. Love.

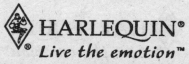

HARLEQUIN®
Live the emotion™

Visit us at www.forrestersquare.com

PHFS3

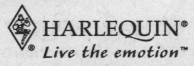

eHARLEQUIN.com

For **FREE online reading,** visit
www.eHarlequin.com now and enjoy:

<u>**Online Reads**</u>
Read **Daily** and **Weekly** chapters from
our Internet-exclusive stories by your
favorite authors.

<u>**Red-Hot Reads**</u>
Turn up the heat with one of our more
sensual online stories!

<u>**Interactive Novels**</u>
Cast your vote to help decide how these
stories unfold...then stay tuned!

<u>**Quick Reads**</u>
For shorter romantic reads, try our
collection of Poems, Toasts, & More!

<u>**Online Read Library**</u>
Miss one of our online reads?
Come here to catch up!

<u>**Reading Groups**</u>
Discuss, share and rave with other
community members!

For great reading online,
visit www.eHarlequin.com today!

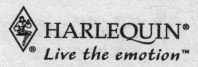

**From Silhouette Books comes
an exciting NEW spin-off to *The Coltons*!**

PROTECTING
PEGGY

by award-winning author
Maggie Price

When FBI forensic scientist
Rory Sinclair checks into
Peggy Honeywell's inn late
one night, the sexy bachelor
finds himself smitten with the
single mother. While Rory works
undercover to solve the mystery
at a nearby children's ranch, his
feelings for Peggy grow...but
will his deception shake the
fragile foundation of their
newfound love?

Coming in December 2003.

THE COLTONS
FAMILY. PRIVILEGE. POWER.

Where love comes alive™